TURNER'S CROSSROADS

Penelope J. Stokes

LIFEJOURNEY
BOOKS

DISCLAIMER

Most works of fiction bear a disclaimer stating that "no character in this work is based on any actual person, living or dead." Such a statement can never be true—any character *not* based in reality has no business appearing in a story. Everyone I've ever met is in this book. You are the noble character. The people you don't like are the villains. *PJS*

LifeJourney Books™ is an imprint of Chariot Family Publishing, a division of David C. Cook Publishing Co.
David C. Cook Publishing Col, Elgin, Illinois 60120
David C. Cook Publishing Co., Weston, Ontario
Nova Distribution Ltd., Newton Abbot, England

TURNER'S CROSSROADS
© 1993 by Penelope J. Stokes

Cover design by Paetzold Design
Cover illustration by Robert Bergin
Interior Design by Glass House Graphics
Edited by Susan Brinner

First Printing, 1993
Printed in the United States of America
97 96 95 94 93 5 4 3 2 1

CIP Applied For
ISBN 0-78140-066-X

Dedication

To my mother,
who instilled in me a love for stories
and who taught me that words can sing;

And to my father,
a spinner of tales,
who gave me a passion for life.

You have invested in my dreams. . .

TURNER'S CROSSROADS

Table
of Contents

Acknowledgements

Many hearts, many lives, many experiences go into the making of stories such as these.

Longtime friends and members of my critique group, Charette Barta, Terry White, Father Jerry Foley, and Lois Walfrid Johnson have given me invaluable editorial assistance, spiritual direction, and personal encouragement. Charette, especially, has been a stalwart in my life. She has believed in my writing from the beginning and helped me discover the vision for my fiction.

Pastor Sharon Worthington and Jackie Ziemer, my faithful prayer partners, have shared with me their struggles, their victories, their dreams, their prayers. They have walked with me both in darkness and in light, and I will ever be grateful for their example of faith.

My pastor, Terry Cathcart, read these stories and laughed in all the right places. Terry has exerted a significant influence in encouraging me to write—and to live—with joyful abandon.

Special thanks are due to two extraordinary editors: to Dave Horton, who caught fire with a vision for this book and faith in my gifts; and to Sue Brinner, whose superior skill and insistent questions snatched me from the flames, saving me from terminal embarrassment. Everyone needs editors—you two are the best.

One other, who prefers to remain nameless, has been of inestimable value to my life and my work, both as friend and as colleague. There is no way to express the depth of my appreciation for all she is and does—but God knows.

Finally, to all the Mansfield Fishers and Sister Gertrudes who have passed through my life, I say "thank you"—for opening my eyes to spiritual reality, for helping me discover the truth of God in all things and the hand of God in all human experience.

❧

Preface

TURNER'S CROSSROADS, squatting directly in the center of six hundred square miles of Midwest farmland, seems to be a town like a thousand other mid-sized towns struggling to survive in the changing Grain Belt. Flanked by the sluggish Blue River to the north and St. Sebaldus Catholic Church to the south, the town is marked like a pirate's treasure where the two rail lines intersect in a perfect X just west of the grain elevator.

Years ago, Turner's Crossroads outgrew its identity as a small town; with a population nearing ten thousand, most of the old timers say it's ninety-five hundred too big. But when the Four Korners Kafe opens and the people of the Crossroads gather for morning coffee, the whole world seems to lurch backward fifty years, and the lines of demarcation are clearly drawn.

The bachelor farmers sit on stools at the counter like ancient crows on a power line, craning their necks to try to hear the conversation at the other end of the row. The guys from American Home Insurance fill one of the booths, while the office workers from Tri-County Electric hover over a table near the window. The loan officer from First Farmers Bank occupies a booth by himself, his back to the wall. And sometimes at the center table, within earshot of all the local gossip, a lone professor from Crossroads Christian College will sit quietly sipping his tea, monitoring the moral standing of the community.

Yet for all their diversity, the citizens of Turner's Crossroads get along remarkably well. United in their resistance to progress and their suspicion of newcomers, they remember with fond pride the "terrible winter of 1849," when their ancestors, with grit and determination, lived through the worst blizzard of the century and, in the spring of 1850, founded Turner's Crossroads. Brought together by the unshakable power of memory, they hold the line against unwelcome change.

Most of the time.

But when Mansfield Fisher moves to town, change comes whether they want it or not.

In Turner's Crossroads, a man is not known by the company he keeps, but by the way he keeps up his property. And Manny Fisher is known as a trasher. He has lived in several different farmhouses around the county, most of which had to be burned to the ground when he left. No one—not even the two single mothers who live with their children in the big

unpainted rental house on the other side of the elevator—wants Manny Fisher anywhere near the pristine
little community of Turner's Crossroads.

Still Manny comes, whether they want him to or
not. He buys the Widow Randolph's lovely little farm-
stead just on the other side of the river, at the junction
of County Roads 18 and 32. Anyone coming into
Turner's Crossroads has to pass Manny's house, and
the old farmers start taking bets on how long it will be
before the place looks like a junkyard.

But Manny surprises them all.

The revelation that Mansfield Fisher's barn brings to
the citizens of Turner's Crossroads is only the beginning of choices and changes, both for the town as a
whole, and for individual citizens. Those decisions,
and their inevitable results, are chronicled in *Turner's
Crossroads.*

These are stories of ordinary people living ordinary
lives, and finding that God is at work in extraordinary
ways among them. The choices they make may not
look like earth-shattering, life-changing decisions, but
they soon discover that God has a way of using the
smallest things in monumental ways.

So it is with all of us. We daily stand at the crossroads, compelled to make decisions. The seemingly
insignificant relationship, the thoughtless word, the
wise or unwise choice, may work in the secret places
of our spirits to determine the course for the rest of
our lives.

Human nature, with all its faults and foibles, prejudices and passions, is nevertheless the glorious cre-
ation of a God whose Spirit is the ultimate reality in

human endeavor. If we have our eyes open, we find that Spirit everywhere—in laughter or in tears, in conflict or in peace. When we learn to laugh at our own folly and weep at our own pathos, God laughs with us and weeps with us...and through the laughter and the tears, clears our vision to enable us to see ourselves as others see us.

❧

Mansfield Fisher and the Revelation Barn

**For the foolishness of God is
wiser than man's wisdom....
—1 Corinthians 1:25**

WHEN WORD came down from On High that Mansfield Fisher had bought the Widow Randolph's place out on the highway, everybody in Turner's Crossroads raised cane. The rumor was reliable, all right: Sylvia Munson, who worked in the County Office of Records and Assessments over in Marshall Forks, knew most of what was bought and sold in Angstrom County, and she broadcast whatever she knew.

"Old Turner Angstrom would turn over in his grave, he would," spat Eddie Bjerke. He set his coffee cup down with a clatter and looked at the familiar weathered faces of the farmers around the center table at the Four Korners Kafe. He knew his sentiment was upheld by most of the citizens in Turner's Crossroads.

"He would," echoed Marvin Angstrom, great-grandson of the revered First Settler in the county. "My grandpa, and his pa before him, worked hard to make this into a town, a respectable town. He wouldn'ta wanted the likes of Fisher to come in bringing his trashy ways."

"Isn't there something we can do?"

"Syl Munson says the papers are all signed and the place is paid for—all legal and done. Guess we're stuck with Manny junking up the place for the next twenty years."

"Unless we convince him to move on." Johnny Leland, one of the few whose family had not settled Angstrom County three generations ago, shifted a toothpick back and forth in the space between his front teeth. He sucked on the chewed-up wood thoughtfully, then pointed it at Marvin. "You remember, we got rid of that welfare thief a few years back—"

"Johnson? Sure, but we had reason to show him the door. He nearly robbed us all blind before that spineless jellyfish of a sheriff got close enough to put the cuffs on him. Fisher's honest enough—and not a bad guy, really."

"He's just odd, that's all. Won't come to church. Hermits himself up. Doesn't talk to anybody."

"And—" Bjerke concluded, putting on his cap and jacket and heading for the door, "he'll have that nice place at the corner of 18 and 32, the first thing anybody sees of the Crossroads, made into a junkyard in three months' time."

🐚

But Mansfield Fisher surprised them all.

Off and on for two weeks, Eddie Bjerke had led a slow-moving caravan of pickup trucks snaking by the intersection of County Roads 18 and 32, just to see what was going on at the Fisher place.

"Can you believe it?" Bjerke said when they had returned to the cafe. "Manny's actually fixing up the place!" He jerked his hands with the force of his words, sloshing his coffee onto the stained green Formica of the table top.

Johnny Leland laughed and poked Bjerke across the table. "Ah, Eddie, you're just sore because he's proving you wrong—you said he'd trash the place."

"Something's happened to Manny," Bjerke said seriously. "I don't know what it is, but it's something."

🐚

It was something, all right. On Sunday, to the shock and disbelief of the entire congregation of St. Thomas Lutheran Church, Mansfield Fisher, scrubbed pink, in clean overalls and a new white shirt, marched up the aisle and sat down in the second row.

The word went forth, whispered, from one row to the next: "Manny Fisher's here...what do you suppose...well, if that isn't something!"

Nobody heard a word of Pastor Logemann's sermon except Manny, who smiled broadly and nodded in agreement at various points. He stood straight and tall in the second row, head thrown back, singing the hymns at the top of his off-key voice.

Near the end of the service, the pastor came down the steps and stood facing the congregation at the head of the center aisle. "I have a blessed duty to perform this morning," he said quietly. "One of our neighbors has come into the fold and wishes to be baptized." He paused. Mansfield Fisher stood up and walked to the front of the church.

Everyone drew in a collective breath as Fisher humbly bent his massive girth and leaned his head down over the baptismal font. In total silence the church waited, hearing the murmured words and the splash of water. At last Manny lifted his balding head and turned to face the congregation, his radiant smile met by looks of incredulity, even hostility.

After the service, Manny stood at the sanctuary entrance with the pastor. Eddie Bjerke tried to escape out the side door, but Pastor Logemann's exuberance wouldn't let him get away. "Isn't it wonderful!" the pastor said, shaking Bjerke's hand and passing him on to Manny, who stood waiting.

"Wonderful," Bjerke muttered, trying to extricate himself from Manny's enthusiastic pumping. At last Bjerke looked up into the shining, moon-shaped face. Fisher was smiling, but his eyes probed into Bjerke's with a look of compassion and knowledge that shook Eddie to his roots. Flustered, Eddie broke free and ran for it.

ख

"It was like—I don't know—like he *knew* something...." Marv Angstrom, like everybody else in the

Four Korners on Monday morning, was talking about the strange effect of Mansfield Fisher's baptismal coming-out.

Eddie Bjerke, relieved that he wasn't the only one who felt it, agreed. "Yeah, he just looked me in the eye and, well, it was like he was looking right through me."

"I think you guys have been out in the sun too long," said Mavis Kitchens, the morning waitress. "He seemed harmless enough to me." She set down a plate of donuts and walked back behind the counter.

"Harmless, maybe," Johnny Leland said. "But we'd better keep an eye on him anyway."

Marv stared hard at Leland. "Who died and made you king?" he snapped.

"Ah, c'mon, Marv," Johnny protested. "Just because your great-grandpa settled here first don't give you the right—"

Marvin shut him up with a look that said, *Remember your place, sonny; your folks have only been around for fifty years.*

As it turned out, everybody was keeping an eye on Mansfield Fisher. Four or five cars a day cruised by on Manny's farm road—in Angstrom County, a regular rush hour.

Then one day, during afternoon coffee at the cafe, Syl Munson walked in and slumped into a booth at the back. "He's done it," she muttered to nobody in particular.

"Who's done what?" Eddie Bjerke said.

She shook her head and waved her hands distractedly. "Manny Fisher's painted his barn."

Marv Angstrom shook his head and mouthed the word *Women!* "Well, now, Syl," he said, "that doesn't seem to be anything to get so depressed about. I mean, after all, we didn't want to see the place junked up—"

Sylvia's head shot up and she glared at Marv venomously. "Go out and see for yourself."

They did. In four pickup trucks, the leaders of Turner's Crossroads made their way down the rutted gravel roads to the intersection of County Roads 18 and 32.

Manny was nowhere in sight. The house, glistening with a fresh coat of white paint, shone like a pearl against the green velvet of the recently mowed lawn. Two of the outbuildings had been painted barn red, and the grove stood like a well-groomed park, completely free of the usual farm litter of old gas engines and worn-out tillers.

Nobody could believe how good the place looked. In silence the men gaped at the transformation, then their eyes focused on the massive barn. Whitewashed, it looked twice its normal size, and across the side in red, clearly visible from the road, the neatly painted words read: *REPENT, FOR THE KINGDOM IS AT HAND.*

"What does he mean, *repent?*" Marv said through gritted teeth.

"Repent means to ask forgiveness, to—" Eddie began. Marv silenced him with a look. He knew very well what the word meant, of course; he and Eddie Bjerke had gone through confirmation class together at St. Thomas Lutheran under old Pastor Gomsrud, back in 1959. But repentance was something you only talked about in church, if at all. It wasn't something you splattered across the side of your barn for the whole world to see. Religion was a private matter, especially in Southern Minnesota. Mansfield Fisher may have "come into the fold," as Pastor Logemann had put it, but if this was his idea of becoming a good Lutheran, he had gone too far.

Nobody said a word on the ride back into town. When they pulled up in front of the Four Korners Kafe, Marv shut off the engine and sat in the truck, still as a statue. Johnny Leland parked next to Marv, got out of his pickup, and came over to Marv's side to lean in the window.

"What're we gonna do about him?" Johnny said.

Marv shook his head. "I don't know. I gotta think about it."

&

In the next few days, Marvin Angstrom thought of little else besides the message written on the side of Mansfield Fisher's barn. The verse worked on him like an incantation, dredging up memories he thought he had buried long ago: the time he had painted over the rust on a used car and sold it to Leif Hanson for full book price; the lies he had told his wife, Addie, the time he had gone to Minneapolis alone for a week.

For the first time in six years, Marv had dreamed of the woman he had met in Minneapolis that week. He was sure, when he turned over the next morning and looked into Addie's eyes, that she knew. She knew, all right; the pain was there, a vacant emptiness he had never seen before. How could he have missed it?

All along, Marv had made excuses when the little twist in his gut told him he was wrong to go out with the woman, wrong to sell a defective car to poor ignorant Leif, wrong to take a tax deduction three years running on the tractor he had traded back to John Deere after the axle got bent.

On those rare occasions when Pastor Logemann had preached about repentance and forgiveness and Marv had listened, he always assumed that the message was for someone else—for Hans Midthun, who drank himself senseless every weekend and went home to beat his wife and kids; for Tennie Hovland, the buxom waitress at the truckstop on the highway, who flaunted her wares and auctioned herself off to the highest bidder. Now, *that* was sin.

But the pastor's sermons didn't apply to Marv. He was a good man, a hard worker. He loved his kids, took care of his wife, lived as decent a life as anybody else. He'd had a few slip-ups in his life; who hadn't? Nobody was perfect. Yet now, because of a few words on the side of a barn, he was being turned inside out with memories he didn't ask for. His sense of well-being was gone, vanished. And it was all Mansfield Fisher's fault.

ès

When Marv Angstrom showed up at the Four Korners Kafe on Thursday, everybody was talking about Mansfield Fisher's barn. Marv didn't want to hear it, but he had to listen anyway. Most of the people in Turner's Crossroads were upset about it, but nobody seemed to be having the kind of trouble Marv was experiencing. Nobody said a word about having old memories surface, about seeing the past come back to haunt them.

When the crowd had thinned and most of the folks had gone back to work, Eddie Bjerke faced Marv across the cafe table and clenched his coffee cup in his hands. He looked directly into Marv's face, his eyes narrowed with intensity.

"Marv," he said, glancing over his shoulder nervously, "we've been friends a long time."

Marv nodded, waiting.

"Well—" Eddie hesitated. "Aw, it's probably just my imagination."

Marv perked up. "Is this about Fisher's barn?"

Eddie stared at him. "How did you know?"

"Never mind. Go on."

"Well," Eddie said, "ever since we saw that message on Manny's barn, things have been going on in my mind—strange things." He paused. "I know this sounds really stupid," he said at last, "and it doesn't sound like me at all, but I've been remembering things, wondering about things that I haven't thought about in years."

Marv nodded. So it wasn't just him!

"I tried to ignore it," Eddie said. "I mean, I'm just as good as the next guy, right? But—" He shook his head. "I just couldn't get it out of my mind: *Repent, for the Kingdom is at hand.*"

"So what did you do?" Marv prodded. He felt sorry for Eddie's misery, but he was glad Eddie was saying this to him, and not the other way around.

"I kept going back out there, every day," Eddie said. "You been out there since Monday?"

Marv shook his head. "No."

"Well, there's more. Tuesday, in addition to the first message, it said: *The wages of sin is death.*"

Marv winced. "And Wednesday?"

"Wednesday he had added, *The pure in heart shall see God.*" Eddie slammed his hand down on the table. "Who does Fisher think he is, anyway—accusing us like that?"

Marv shook his head. "I don't know, but..."

Eddie stared hard at his friend, a light of understanding dawning in his eyes. "Ah," he said. "So you've felt it, too."

Marv was caught, and he knew it. "Yeah," he muttered. "Ever since the first message, I've been remembering a lot of stuff I've done wrong over the years."

"Me, too." Eddie heaved a sigh of relief, glad that the truth was out.

Silence hung between them for a moment. "You know what, Eddie?" Marv said at last.

"What?"

"For the last couple of days I've been mad, real mad, at Manny for putting that stuff up on his barn for everybody to see. It was like he had written all my secrets in plain view. I coulda killed him. But now with what you're telling me about the rest of it, about the pure in heart seeing God, I wonder if maybe the messages are coming from—well, from somewhere else."

"From God?" Eddie couldn't keep the sneer out of his voice.

"Maybe." Marv averted his eyes. He played with the spoon until it clattered noisily to the table.

"Eddie," Marv said finally, "do you suppose other people are feeling the same way?"

"I don't know," Eddie said. "People around here don't talk much about religion."

"Yeah, yeah," Marv said. "I know. It's a private matter. But Manny's sure making it public. He's forcing people to think about their lives, and nobody's very happy about it, far as I can see."

❧

The following Sunday, you could have heard a pin drop in St. Thomas Lutheran Church. Even the children were quiet, riveted to their seats as if waiting for something to happen.

Mansfield Fisher took his seat on the second row, and a hundred pairs of eyes bored into the back of his skull. He didn't seem to notice. He smiled and nodded and sang the hymns at the top of his off-key voice.

Pastor Logemann stood up to give his sermon. "My text for this morning comes from Matthew, chapter five, verse eight: 'Blessed are the pure in heart, for they shall see God.'"

Eddie Bjerke's head snapped around and his eyes fixed on Marv Angstrom, three rows back. Marv was staring straight at Pastor Logemann, his face blizzard-white, a sheen of sweat across his brow. The pastor spoke in quiet tones for a few moments about the necessity of forgiveness. Then he came down and stood in the center of the aisle, where a week before

Mansfield Fisher had been baptized.

"We're going to do something this morning that we rarely do in the Lutheran church—and maybe we should do it more often. Before we come to communion, we always have a time of silence and reflection, a time for repentance of sin. This morning I'm going to ask any of you who wish to make that repentance public to come up to the altar to pray. None of us is perfect; we all have need of forgiveness. But if we want to be pure in heart, and be able to see God at work in our lives, we need to begin by being honest with him."

The pastor returned to his seat, and Lavonne Amundson began to play hymns softly on the organ. Nobody moved; nobody even breathed. Then, after three full minutes of total stillness, a shifting of hymnbooks and purses and papers began to ripple through the sanctuary. Pastor Logemann got up from his seat and went to kneel at the communion rail. Everybody watched, amazed, as his shoulders slumped and then gently began to shake. He was crying!

Eddie Bjerke shot another look back at the Angstroms. Marv didn't see him; he had hold of Addie's hand and was leaning toward her, whispering. The two of them got up and went slowly forward to the rail.

Eddie closed his eyes and breathed deeply, trying to steady himself. For a fleeting moment he considered joining them; something inside of him prodded him to get up, but he fought against it. Whatever he might have felt when he saw the messages on Mansfield Fisher's barn, he had to get a grip on himself.

Religion, after all, was a private matter.

When he looked up again, the altar rail was nearly full, and people were milling up and down the aisle. On the back row, a few stony-faced women glared at the spectacle, then got up and stalked out the back door. Eddie shook his head. He felt embarrassed, ashamed for Marv Angstrom and all these other fools who were letting their emotions run away with them.

Eddie watched. Marv and Addie Angstrom came back down the aisle past him, smiling, and resumed their seats. In a few minutes it was all over. When the communion liturgy began and Lavonne hit the opening chords for "This Is the Feast of Victory for Our God," Mansfield Fisher's off-key voice was drowned out by the volume of a hundred other voices.

❧

That afternoon, after Sunday dinner and the newspaper, Marvin Angstrom took his wife for a drive in the country. They happened to pass by the Fisher place and stopped to read the barn. All the previous verses had been painted over and, across the side of the whitewashed wall, one message stood out: *THOUGH YOUR SINS BE AS SCARLET, THEY SHALL BE WHITE AS SNOW.*

Manny stood in the driveway, still dressed in his Sunday overalls and white shirt. He waved, then turned and went back in the house.

❧

Word got around quickly about the odd goings-on

at the church in Turner's Crossroads. The Four Korners Kafe was crowded to capacity at nine o'clock Monday morning, and the conversation, as expected, centered around Mansfield Fisher's barn.

A lot of the people in outlying areas hadn't seen the barn for themselves; they had only heard the rumors. At ten, a line of cars that looked like a funeral procession for the governor rounded the curve at the intersection of County Roads 18 and 32.

The house, glistening with a fresh coat of white paint, shone like a pearl against the green velvet of the recently mowed lawn. The grove resembled a well-groomed park. Everyone was impressed with how beautifully kept up the place was.

And there, across the driveway from the house, stood the barn. Whitewashed, it looked twice its normal size. A dozen newcomers got out of their cars and hung on the open doors, staring.

The reports that filtered back in to the Four Korners Kafe on Monday afternoon varied. Some said there were no messages at all on the barn; others described elaborate paintings of the Four Horsemen of St. John's Revelation. One man claimed to see the face of Jesus on the barn door.

Eddie Bjerke drove out one last time to see for himself. The barn was whitewashed; all the messages were gone. He parked his pickup on the side of County Road 32 and sat for an hour, a sense of loss and loneliness overwhelming him. By the time he started his truck and headed back toward Turner's Crossroads, he had convinced himself that it had all been a figment of his imagination.

It was dangerous, this religious fervor. It made people imagine things about themselves, doubt what they knew was true. He wasn't such a bad guy, after all. He wasn't perfect, of course; but who was?

Right then and there, on the road back into Turner's Crossroads, Eddie made his decision. Next Sunday he would go out to North Creek Church, where people believed that religion was a private matter.

ॐ

Hostage Child

**First go and be reconciled...then come
and offer your gift."
—Matthew 5:24**

S HEILA JORGENSON jerked awake, trembling.
The sheets were damp with sweat, her muscles
knotted and sore. The dream had come again,
and this time she remembered it. She wished she
could forget.

Sheila drew a terrycloth bathrobe around her to
ward off the cold, but it didn't help. The chill came
from within, shuddering outward in waves of fear and
helplessness.

She stumbled to the kitchen and went through the
motions of making coffee, then took a cup into the
dimly lit dining room and slumped down at the table.

Through the east windows she could see the first gray light of dawn. But no sunrise could lift the heavy weight in her heart.

Bear was gone again, as he often was these days, driving an eighteen-wheeler for Harteland Trucking out to the West Coast and back again. Sheila smiled briefly at the thought of her burly, bearded, teddy-bear of a husband. He was doing his best to make ends meet, and she did love him for it. But somehow he never seemed to be in town when the inevitable catastrophes of life crashed down upon her. She needed him now, and she wished desperately that he were here.

☙

The dream had come, as always, in three stages. In the first scene, Sheila saw a young girl on the back porch of a dilapidated farmhouse. Dressed in hand-me-down jeans, the child sat on the steps, laughing, playing with a new litter of barn kittens. The mother rubbed up against her legs as the little ones pounced on her bare toes and made flying leaps into the air to attack a passing butterfly.

Suddenly the screen door flew open and a tall, ominous figure filled the doorway. Although she could not see the face shrouded in shadow, Sheila knew instinctively that it was the child's father. Behind him, grabbing at his arm and shouting, a pale, haggard woman in a blue print housedress desperately tried to get the man back into the house.

The man pointed a bony finger and stumbled across the threshold. "I'm gonna drown them blasted cats!" he yelled. He pulled his arm away. "Let me go, woman!"

Lunging toward the litter, he grabbed a yowling kitten in each hand and shook them in the child's face, then turned and plunged them into the huge barrel of rainwater at the corner of the house.

The little girl jumped to her feet and grabbed the man's arm. "Daddy, don't! Don't!" she sobbed.

"Get out of my way!" He flung his arm back against her, sending the child reeling into the dirt. In the midst of her dream, Sheila could feel the force of the blow, smell the pungent odor of whiskey on his breath.

She was the little girl, and the angry, drunken man was her father.

The child Sheila, still crying, began to get up; her bare foot pushed against a wet, lifeless mass. In terror, she looked down at the scraggly, drowned kitten, then up again into her father's eyes. A rage burned there, a look that said, *You're next.*

And Sheila the child jumped to her feet and ran, across the ridged rows of plowed field, through the corn stubble that cut her bare feet, toward the safety of her grandmother's house a mile away.

The child Sheila ran and ran, her heart pumping wildly. In the distance through the grove she could just see Gramma Langstrom's house. Relief flooded over her; once she reached the enfolding comfort of Gramma's hug, she would be safe! She closed her eyes and took a deep breath.

But when she opened them again, the scene had shifted. No longer was Sheila a child; no longer was she approaching her grandmother's house. Instead, she came out of the woods into the parking lot of the SuperSave grocery store.

The liquor store next to the SuperSave was surrounded by police cars, their lights flashing. Men in uniforms trained their guns on the door of the liquor store, and an official-looking man with a bullhorn was calling, "COME ON OUT BEFORE SOMEONE GETS HURT!"

"What's going on?" Sheila asked a uniformed officer nearby.

"Some nut is in the liquor store with a gun, holding three people hostage," the man explained tersely.

Sheila squinted toward the glass front of the liquor store. A tall man in khaki pants stood in the doorway, his pistol jammed against the temple of a middle-aged woman—a pale, haggard woman in a blue print housedress. "I'll let 'em all go!" the man screamed. "Just send her in!" He extended his left arm and pointed directly at Sheila.

Somehow, in the dream, Sheila knew what she must do. She laid her purse on the nearest police car and walked as calmly as she could toward the door of the liquor store. "I'm coming," she called loudly, her voice trembling. "Let them go."

As Sheila reached the entrance, the three panic-stricken hostages loomed before her in the doorway. The woman stood aside and urged the other hostages—two young boys—to safety. In the final moment of the exchange, Sheila's eyes locked with the woman's. The expression she saw wrenched her heart—an expression of helplessness, of futility, a familiar, pained, haunted look.

The woman reached up a rough, work-worn hand and touched Sheila's cheek briefly. "I'm sorry," she whispered. Then she was gone.

Sheila opened the door and looked into the blazing, bloodshot eyes of her father.

She didn't know how long she remained a hostage in the liquor store. But finally, somehow, she was released. She opened the door to go out into the sunshine and stepped instead into a dark, close room with candles burning and soft music playing.

It was a funeral parlor. Before her lay an open casket; all she could see of the body was the pale, bony hands clasped over the chest. The fingers looked like wax castings, not at all human, but somehow familiar. Sheila knew. She didn't need to look, didn't want to look; yet something propelled her toward the coffin, her footsteps silent on the cushioned carpeting.

Sheila's breath caught in her chest. With a jerk, the body sat up and turned its waxen countenance in her direction. The eyes blazed, and a gaunt finger shot up and pointed toward her.

Sheila opened her mouth to scream, but no sound came. Then she woke up, shaking and gasping for breath.

❧

The coffee in her cup had grown cold. Sheila tasted it, grimaced, and put it down again. The sun had risen, and outside the dining room window she could hear the sounds of the day coming to life—a dog's bark, the rattling bicycle of the paper boy as he made his rounds in the north end of Turner's Crossroads.

Somewhere a child laughed, and music from a radio drifted across the yard and in the open window.

Sheila put her head in her hands and sighed. "Dear God," she murmured, "what am I going to do?"

The dream was all too real, its implications all too clear. Her father was dying, failing fast from the effects of a lifetime of alcoholism, and there was nothing—nothing—Sheila could do about it.

The county social worker had called yesterday to inform Sheila that something *had* to be done about Arlen Langstrom. He was driving again, and someone in town had complained. Sheila and her brothers had gone out to the farmhouse to see him. He was barely able to walk from his chair in the living room to the bathroom and back again, and yet he insisted that he would not leave his house and go into the nursing home. When they had tried to reason with him, he turned mean.

"Get out!" he had screamed. "You ain't putting me in no home! All of you—get out! And don't come back here again!"

Beaten, they had left. Sheila had pocketed his keys on the way out of the house. He would be furious, but she had no choice.

Now she sat at her dining room table, trying to pray, trying to sort out the dream from the reality. She loved her father, and she hated him. She wanted him to live, but she knew, ashamed, that she would feel only relief when he was finally dead. And the last scene of her dream haunted her. Would he, once dead, still accuse her from his grave?

Sheila shook her head. The dream was absurd, a

fiction concocted in the night by her own pain and stress. Her father had never drowned kittens; he had never hit her, or pointed a gun at her. He had never abused her brothers—only ignored them. He had tried to be a decent father, she supposed, when his mind was not clouded by drink. And she had done all she could to be a dutiful daughter. But they had never, never had a normal family life.

Maybe she just needed to try harder.

❧

At three that afternoon, Sheila drove the eleven miles out into the country to the farmhouse. Just pulling into the gravel driveway took her back to her childhood, to those early days when she would, as in her dream, run barefoot across the fields to Gramma Langstrom's house. She could close her eyes and hear the lowing of cows at milking time, smell the heavy, sweet scents of horse feed and leather, feel the wooly softness of new lambs. Life on the farm should have been a joyous, untroubled childhood. But she remembered only her mother's care-lined face, the weary expression, the infrequent smile that never quite reached her mother's eyes.

Sheila sighed and got out of the car.

The front door of the house sagged open on its hinges. On the kitchen table, amid the litter of overflowing ashtrays and week-old newspapers, a depleted bottle lay on its side.

The garage stood empty. Her father must have hidden another set of keys. His truck was gone.

ક

Sheila saw the battered old Chevy pickup as soon as she pulled into the parking lot at the Last Chance Tavern. Around the doorway, two police cars were parked at odd angles, their lights flashing.

Sheila pushed her way into the darkened tavern and grabbed at the uniformed policeman standing in the doorway. It was Tick Restin; she had known him since high school. "What's happened?" she demanded.

"Some old guy. Been here drinking since just before noon, the bartender said. He collapsed, and they called us. Ambulance is on the way."

Sheila's eyes strained to adjust to the dim light, and at last she saw him, lying on the dirty floor next to the bar. Gaunt and unshaven, with two days' growth of gray stubble on the sagging flesh of his face and neck, he lay motionless, like a rag doll dropped to the ground by a distracted child. One leg was folded under the body, and his right arm stuck out straight, twisted crazily at the elbow.

Sheriff Ferrel knelt over him.

"Daddy!" Sheila ran to him, shoving through the crowd, and fell on her knees next to him.

"Sheila Jorgenson!" the sheriff said. "Is this your father?"

Sheila nodded. "He's Arlen Langstrom."

"I never would have recognized him."

"Is he—"

"He's alive," the sheriff said curtly. "But just barely." Ferrel turned to Restin, still standing in the doorway. "Where's that ambulance?"

"Unit's just pulling up," Tick said, glancing over his shoulder. He nodded toward Sheila. "You want to ride with him?"

ଈ

All the way to the hospital, and later, in the waiting room while the doctors in ICU worked on her father, Sheila could think of nothing but the terror of seeing those flashing lights in front of the Last Chance Tavern. She sat, staring numbly, but no tears came. At last she lay down on the couch in the visitor's lounge and fell into an exhausted, fitful sleep.

Again she dreamed. This time, instead of the incident at the farm or the funeral home scene, she saw only the parking lot of the SuperSave, the doorway of the liquor store, the red and blue lights of the police cars flashing, flashing....

Then she was inside the store, facing her father's blazing, bloodshot eyes. In his hand he held not a gun, but a bottle. And—why had she not noticed this before?—behind him, hidden in the shadows of the crates, stood another figure, still as death, with the light gleaming off the steel-blue barrel of a pistol.

Her father was whispering in low, urgent tones, "We've gotta get out of here. We've gotta get out!"

They were both hostages.

ଈ

An insistent hand shook Sheila awake. Bending over her, his stethoscope dangling in front of his chest, stood a short, balding man in a white coat. The name tag on his breast pocket read *Randolph Carter, M.D.*

"Miss Langstrom?"

Sheila squinted up at him. "It's Jorgenson. Sheila Jorgenson. My maiden name was Langstrom."

"Yes, of course," the doctor stammered. "Your father. You'd better come now."

"Is he all right?"

"He's awake. But his kidneys and liver have failed. He won't be with us for long, I'm afraid." The doctor shook his head and helped Sheila to her feet. "I'm sorry, Mrs. Jorgenson. There was simply nothing we could do."

Sheila nodded and followed him down the hall.

Through the glass door of ICU, Sheila observed the still figure of a man, covered by a thin blanket. From her vantage point at the door, all she could see of him was a pair of gaunt, pale hands folded over his chest. Her footsteps made soft clicking noises on the tile floor as she approached the bed.

Her father's eyes, sunken and smudged with dark circles, were closed. For a long time Sheila stood there looking at him, saying nothing. At last, almost involuntarily, she breathed, "Oh, Daddy!"

The eyes snapped open, and the head turned toward the sound. Sheila shrank back, but a withered, clawlike hand reached out and grabbed at her wrist. His touch was cold, and she shuddered.

He opened his mouth to speak. "Sheila," he whispered

"I'm here, Daddy." Tears welled up in Sheila's eyes, and she choked back the lump in her throat. She squeezed the bony hand gently.

"I...never meant..." he began, then his breath gave out, and he wheezed. The sound made Sheila's chest hurt. "I just never could manage to give it up...the drinking, I mean."

"Don't try to talk, Daddy," Sheila said, her own voice cracking.

"I gotta say this—" His words dissolved into a fit of coughing. When he regained his breath, he continued. "All these years, I've been in prison...it was a jail I made for myself. You understand?"

"I understand, Daddy." Sheila's mind flashed to the insistent image of herself and her father being held at gunpoint by a shadowed, unknown figure in the back of the liquor store. "We were both hostages."

He nodded weakly. "Do you think God'll forgive me?"

Sheila's tears spilled over. "I think so, Daddy." She waited, holding her breath, hoping for the words she had longed for all her life: *Forgive me* or *I love you*. Something—anything....

But the words did not come.

The dutiful daughter inside of her formed instinctive words of denial: *There's nothing to forgive; he couldn't help himself.* But it was a lie, and she knew it. There was a lot to forgive—years of pain and anguish and abandonment, a lifetime of having her dreams drowned like innocent, helpless kittens.

If he would only admit the hurt he had caused; if he would only ask for forgiveness, she might be able to grab hold of her faith long enough to find some point of connection with him, some reconciliation. She couldn't *finish* forgiving him now, at this moment. It would take a long time, perhaps as long as the hurt had taken. But she might *begin*—if only he would ask.

The claw clamped down on her hand, and he raised his head from the pillow. His clouded eyes fixed upon hers, and he licked his parched lips as if he intended to speak again. But with one ragged intake of breath, the fire died. The life went out of his eyes, his jaw sagged, and his hand went limp in hers.

Instead of the longed-for words of reconciliation, Sheila heard only the death rattle in her father's throat. It was over—finally, completely over.

As Sheila turned to go, a weight came down on her shoulder. She whirled around to see Bear staring down at her, an expression of pain and love in his eyes. His arms went around her, and she sagged against him and cried. For a long time she stood there, drawing strength from his closeness, feeling the comforting softness of his beard against her forehead.

When she finally looked up, she saw her brothers standing behind the glass wall of ICU, watching....

❧

The night after the funeral, when everyone had gone home and the house was quiet, Sheila tried in vain to warm herself against Bear's great bulk. For a while she cried quietly, ashamed because her tears were not for her father, but for herself, for her own disappointment. When her tears were spent, she tried to pray, to find a pocket of comfort in the midst of her despair. But her mind raced relentlessly, distracting her with snatches of present pain and persistent memory. Finally she gave up and fell into a restless slumber, lulled to sleep by the rhythmic growling of her husband's familiar snore.

And Sheila dreamed again.

On the steps of the dilapidated farmhouse where she had grown up, a little girl sat, her bare feet dangling in the dust. It was nearly sunset, and the dreaming Sheila could see the cows coming in from the pasture, hear the clink of the tin pails as someone in the barn rattled around preparing for milking.

Sheila knew the child was herself. From her place on the steps, she could smell the pork roast Mama was cooking for supper and feel the last warm rays of sunshine on the worn earth around the porch.

Like a black paper cutout against the setting sun, a tall, gaunt figure came from the barn. He walked directly up to the child Sheila and stood towering over her, his muddy workboots looming large in her limited field of vision. His left hand held a full pail of milk; his right was stuffed into his jacket pocket.

Terrified, the child looked up, and up, and up until she saw the craggy face shadowed in the dim light of dusk.

"Found something in the barn," he said shortly. His right hand came out of his pocket and extended toward her. A gray tabby kitten with wide blue eyes stared at Sheila from the outstretched hand. The kitten mewed softly, and a dribble of fresh milk fell off its chin onto the man's long fingers.

"For me?" the child Sheila said, her voice wavering.

He nodded. "Take good care of her, now."

The girl jumped up and gathered the furry bundle into her arms. "I will, Daddy. I will!"

The man reached out and scratched the kitten under its chin. A hint of a smile flickered across his stubbled features. The cat purred and thrust its head into the crook of the child's elbow. "Now," he said, patting the child on the shoulder, "come on in to dinner. It's getting chilly; too cold for you to be out here with no shoes."

The child struggled to her feet, holding the kitten carefully in both arms. She followed her father into the house, and Sheila awoke, smiling, to the slamming of the screen door behind them.

🐾

Miss Nasty's
Sweet Revenge

And there was a widow in that town who kept coming...with the plea, 'Grant me justice against my adversary....'"
—Luke 18:3

FROM A second-story window high above the corner of Fourth and Main, Miss Natalia Paisley pulled back the lace curtain and glared down at the sidewalk. There he was again, Doc Robert Henley, squat and bow-legged, holding one end of the leash while his squat, bow-legged dog lifted its leg against the corner of Miss Natalia's white picket fence.

Natalia's scowl deepened as she heard the clatter of a stick against the pickets. She peered to the left and caught a glimpse of Inky Munson, the grubby little urchin who lived across the alley, barreling down the sidewalk on his bicycle, rattling her pickets with a long narrow branch. Inky skidded to a halt in front of Doc Henley, slammed his bike up against the fence, and jumped down to scratch the pug Churchill under his double chin.

"Hiya, Doc," the boy said amiably, his voice rising clearly on the morning air. "How's old Churchill today?" This last comment was addressed to the dog, not the man, and Churchill responded by rolling compliantly onto his side to have his belly scratched. From her window, Natalia could see the fleshy circle of Doc Henley's bald head leaning over the pale oval of the dog's fat underside—a rounded exclamation point.

"Yep," Doc Henley was saying, "Old Churchill's a champion, you know—championship bloodlines on both sides. His true name is *Churchill's Magnificent Legacy*, sired by *Otto the Magnificent* out of *Festival's Lady Legacy*."

It was what he told everyone, every time, but no one alerted him to the fact that he was repeating himself. Doc Henley was, after all, somewhat of a legend in Turner's Crossroads—the man who singlehandedly delivered most of the longtime residents, their children, and their grandchildren. During the Great Thanksgiving Blizzard of '38, when Mrs. Ettie Duncan had gone into labor out on the farm, Doc had strapped on snowshoes and trudged the four miles out there with a kerosene lantern in one hand and his medical bag in the other. The child was breach, and if it hadn't been for the Doc, who was then only nineteen and fresh out of medical training, both Ettie and her boy would have died.

But Ettie survived and named her son after the green young doctor who saved them both. Only Ettie got the name wrong. In the pain and delirium of her labor, she thought he'd said "Doc Henry," so that's what she named the boy. Last year Henry Duncan had run for mayor and almost won. Natalia often thought he'd be in City Hall today if only his name had been Henley.

Miss Natalia was practically the only person in Turner's Crossroads who didn't think Doc was wonderful. She considered that since *he* thought he was wonderful, he didn't really need the adulation of everybody else in town. But he got it anyway. Doc Henley was the undisputed Grand Old Man of Turner's Crossroads; people stopped on the sidewalk to admire his yard and his prize-winning Glorious Day roses, to give homage to his champion pug Churchill, to bask in the reflected glory of his presence.

Doc, of course, received the veneration of his subjects with all dignity and humility. And loved every minute of it.

❧

Miss Natalia let the curtain drop back into place. She refused to watch that beast Churchill finish his business on the corner of her lawn, refused to give audience to Henley's parting benediction over young Inky Munson. The man was insufferable; why couldn't anyone else see it?

Natalia sighed and sank into one of the wine-colored velvet chairs. The ornate poster bed, the Martha Washington spread, the lace sheers at the window, the tiny roses on the wallpaper—everything was exactly as it had always been; a little worn by time, a little dimmed by sameness, but familiar, comforting.

This room had belonged to her grandmother, the matriarch Victoria Hunter. Here Little Nattie had always come for security and consolation, to have her childish tears dried, her scraped knees bandaged. Everyone else had known Granny Vic as a stern, tyrannical family ruler, center of her own universe, holding them all in the powerful gravity of her will. Only to Nattie had Granny Vic revealed her "secret self," as she called it. With Nattie, the youngest granddaughter, Granny had been tender and loving, ready to listen, ready to tell the stories of her wild and reckless youth. Only Granny Vic had been there for Natalia.

But even Granny Vic couldn't live forever. Hunter Hall, this grand old Gothic house, now belonged to Natalia Paisley. She had kept it exactly the same, a shrine to a bygone era, a monument to the past—her past, Granny Vic's past.

❧

Hearing the chink of Churchill's dog tags, Natalia raised her head. Doc Henley had apparently made it around the block and was headed home. His patterns were predictable; four times a day, he and that obnoxious waddling beast paraded up the walk and around the block like the King and his Consort, bowing and waving to the servile multitudes. Henley loved the veneration of the people. And Churchill, apparently, adored her picket fence.

Through the open window, Natalia heard Doc's gravelly voice and rose from the chair to peer through the curtain lace. Inky Munson was back.

"Say, Doc," Inky said at the top of his high-pitched pre-adolescent voice, "doesn't Miss Nasty get mad at you and Churchill?" The boy laughed, pointing to the dog, who was making one final territorial mark on the corner fencepost. "I mean, if we even come near her precious property, she yells at us from the window up there—" He pointed languidly at the bedroom window, and Natalia shrank back a little from the curtain.

She could see Doc's shoulders bounce as he flung back his head in a hearty laugh. "Well, son," he answered, "I don't know; she's never said. But," he finished, tugging at Churchill's leash and heading for the corner, "I've always lived by the principle, *Never mess on your own front yard.* And the State Fair is coming up in another three weeks. We couldn't have Churchill watering my prize roses, now could we?" Shaking with laughter, he crossed the street and headed toward his house, waving good-bye to Inky Munson as he went.

Natalia pounded her hand down on the bedside table, catching Granny Vic's amethyst ring in the crocheted doily and nearly upsetting the crystal lamp. Miss Nasty, was it? Well, she had had enough— enough of this blatant disregard for her property and her privacy, enough of Doc Henley's dog and Inky Munson's disrespect.

She stomped downstairs, jerked up the telephone, and dialed the sheriff's office.

"But Miss Nas—uh—Miss Natalia," the officer

stammered when she registered her complaint. "There's no law against walking a dog in Turner's Crossroads. And as for the animal's, ah, calling card—"

Natalia could hear him covering the receiver with his hand and trying not to laugh. "Well," he finished when he had regained control, "there's simply no statute that will allow me to arrest an animal for doing what comes naturally." The officer took a deep breath and steadied himself. I'm sorry, Miss Natalia," he said in his best professional voice. "You'll just have to talk to Doc Henley for yourself. He's a reasonable man. Just explain your problem, and—"

Natalia slammed down the receiver. "*My* problem, is it? The Great Doctor has no respect for private property, and it's *my* problem!"

Then, as the white flash of her anger began to subside, an idea presented itself to Miss Natalia Paisley— not fully formed, but gradually, like a picture taking shape on a photographic negative. By the time the image had developed, Miss Nasty was smiling—a secretive, satisfied smile. "What's good for the goose," she murmured to herself, and slipped quietly out the back door to the garage.

ॐ

All the junior officers in the Sheriff's Department hated drawing duty for night rounds. By ten-thirty, most of the lights in Turner's Crossroads were out and people were asleep. Calls that came in to the night desk usually involved a loud cat fight in an alley or, on occasion, a minor ruckus at the Last

Chance Tavern up on the highway.

Tonight promised to be no different. Tick Restin yawned and tried to stay awake as he drove his prowl car up and down the appointed route. Twenty-one and fresh out of law enforcement training, Tick had envisioned a life of high-speed chases and dangerous drug busts in the back streets of a teeming, sleepless city. He had also hoped to escape his childhood nickname, given to him by a thoughtless uncle who told his father, "He'll never amount to more than a tick in a hound's ear." The name had stuck, and the prophecy itself seemed to be coming true.

Instead of chasing criminals on the streets of San Francisco, Tick Restin had ended up back in Turner's Crossroads, where he had grown up, where he himself had spent one cold and miserable night in jail after getting a little out of control at his own graduation party.

The older guys—particularly Sheriff Jake Ferrel, who had been his dad's best friend—had never let Tick live down the memory of being carried into the cell, clad only in his red boxer shorts, after the duty officers dragged him out of the fountain at the Blue River Country Club. Now, whenever Tick protested at being assigned grub duty, someone would haul out the infamous red shorts from a file drawer and threaten to run them up the flagpole.

As he maneuvered the sharp corner at Fourth and Manchester, Tick's heartbeat quickened. There! In the shadows, he could just make out the dark shape of a human figure moving furtively across the narrow strip of lawn between Doc Henley's house and the

Carlsons' driveway. Quickly he scanned the windows in Doc's house. Seeing no sign of light, he snatched up the radio transmitter. "This is Restin. I'm on Fourth and Manchester. Got a prowler at Doc Henley's. Send Dave for a back-up."

Grabbing his flashlight and drawing his gun, Tick crouched into the shadow of the house and followed the dark form around the corner. He caught a whiff of something—a vaguely familiar, harshly acidic smell.

In the darkness behind the house, a darker shadow moved.

"Freeze!" Tick shouted, his voice shaky. He trained the powerful flashlight on the figure and moved closer.

"Miss—Miss Natalia?"

Natalia Paisley stood in the glare of the spotlight, one hand thrown up to shield her eyes, the other holding a large plastic jug. She wore a dark jumpsuit and dangling pearl earrings, and her face wore an expression not of apprehension or dismay, but of defiance.

A second patrol car wheeled to a stop at the curb, its blue and red lights flashing across the darkness. Lights began to come on in the neighboring houses, curtains parted, porch doors opened. Doc Henley's house remained dark.

Dave Sheppard called to Tick as he approached. "What's the problem here?"

Tick's head swiveled around, his gun and flashlight still pointed toward Miss Natalia. "Uh, vandalism, I guess," he stammered.

Dave shook his head and smiled. "I think you can

put away your piece now, sport. She's not likely to resist arrest."

Tick looked down at his gun. He felt his face flush and silently blessed the darkness and the cool night air. "I—I had no way of knowing—"

"Course not, sport," Dave said, slapping him on the shoulder and grinning. An image flashed through Tick's mind—a picture of Notorious Natalia's mug shot, pinned to the department's bulletin board beside his red boxer shorts. He sighed and holstered his weapon.

"Now, what have we here?" Dave said, turning to Natalia and taking the plastic jug out of her hand. He sniffed at the mouth of the jug and grimaced. "Weed killer."

Her spine ramrod-straight, Miss Natalia lifted her chin and glared at him. "Poetic justice," she said.

🙶

Shortly after daybreak, Sheriff Ferrel, accompanied by Tick and Dave, stood in Doc Henley's yard assessing the damage and jotting notes on a clipboard.

"It's a mess, all right," the sheriff said. All over the front lawn, Doc Henley's lush green grass showed large yellow circles. The carefully-clipped shrubs along the walk were beginning to shrivel, and out back, the prize-winning Glorious Day roses drooped woefully.

"Looks like the Glorious Days are headed for a not-so-glorious night," Dave quipped. "The big sleep. Off to Rose Heaven."

"Shut up, Sheppard," the sheriff muttered, jerking his ball-point pen toward Doc Henley. The old man stood on the porch with Churchill at his side, shaking his head miserably.

"Natalia Paisley?" Doc said. They had been through it a dozen times, but the Doc didn't seem to be able to comprehend what the sheriff had told him. "Miss Natalia did this?"

"Miss Nasty's earned her name this time," Dave said. The sheriff shot him a withering glance.

"Tick here caught her in the act," the sheriff repeated patiently.

"But why? Why me? Why my yard, my roses?"

"She wouldn't say. Kept repeating some nonsense about 'poetic justice' and 'what's good for the goose is good for the gander.' Something like that." The sheriff paused, biting on the end of his pen. "Doc," he mused, "do you think the old girl's finally snapped? I mean, living in that big old house all alone for so many years—"

Doc Henley chewed thoughtfully on his thumbnail. "Where is she?"

The sheriff cleared his throat and grinned sheepishly. "At home, I guess. I mean, it didn't seem right to put her in jail. We figured—"

"That's fine," Doc said absently. He opened the screen door and let Churchill into the house, then turned to go in himself.

"Doc?" the sheriff said. "Don't you want to sign this complaint form?" He held out the clipboard and pen.

Doc dismissed him with a wave of the hand. "Not now, Jake," he said. "I need to think about this some more." He turned and went into the house, shutting the door in the sheriff's face.

ঙ

Barely awake after a restless night and a troubled sleep, Natalia heard a movement on the lawn below her bedroom window. She raised her head and peered groggily through the lace curtains to the yard below.

At the corner of the sidewalk she saw the fleshy circle of a bald head, bending low along the fenceline as if looking for something in the grass. Natalia's mind suddenly snapped to attention. Doc Henley!

She slipped out of bed and pulled on her robe, squinting at the clock: six-thirty. The man must be up to no good to come out at the crack of dawn.

Natalia had lain awake most of the night expecting a knock at the door, a telephone call, a summons of some kind. But no such summons had come. Had he decided to retaliate in kind for the loss of his precious roses?

Fuming, Natalia stomped down the stairs and flung open the front door. Doc had his back to her, still doing whatever he was doing—on *her* property, in broad daylight! She took a step forward onto the porch, and almost tripped and fell.

There, on the doormat, sat a huge vase of the most beautiful roses Natalia had ever seen—long-stemmed, fragrant, perfect Glorious Day roses. *Looks like I missed a few,* she thought cynically. *Well, he's not going to get by that easily; he may be able to charm everyone else in this town, but—*

Her thoughts were interrupted by the arrival of Inky Munson, who jumped off his bike and squatted down beside the Doc for a moment, then rolled the bicycle off the sidewalk and propped it against a tree in the boulevard. It was rather like watching a silent movie, and she longed desperately for the subtitles. What in the world was that old fool doing?

Doc Henley pointed, handed something to Inky, and then once more bent his head down toward the ground.

Suddenly he stood up, and her heart gave a leap. She sank deeper into the shadow of the doorway and watched as Doctor Robert Henley lifted a brush and began to apply white paint to the corner post of the picket fence.

Without warning, her eyes clouded with tears and a painful lump caught in her throat.

No one saw her step back into the house, wiping her eyes on the sleeve of her robe. No one saw the door open again as she retrieved the vase of flowers and stood next to the window, breathing in their sweetness and watching with awe the transformation taking place outside.

No one saw. But when Doc Henley turned back and looked toward the porch, his Glorious Day roses had disappeared.

☙

The Charlatan

**My word...will not return to me empty, but will
accomplish what I desire and achieve the
purpose for which I sent it."
—Isaiah 55:11**

SIMON MOUNTBANK screeched his new Cadillac
Seville to a stop in front of the billboard and
leaned back, heaving a deep sigh of satisfaction.
Johnny Baptisto deserved a bonus this time; he was
one PR man who really knew how to do a job right.

Simon craned his head back and looked up into his
own smiling face, ten times larger than life, splashed
across the billboard with the words:

**HEALING for the sick,
HOPE for the weary,
HEAVEN for the sinner....**

**FULL GOSPEL REVIVAL MEETINGS,
APRIL 1-14, 7 p.m. nightly
CROSSROADS HIGH SCHOOL GYMNASIUM**

Johnny had done his job, all right. Beginning tomorrow night, the folks in Turner's Crossroads and surrounding communities wouldn't know what hit 'em.

Simon gunned the engine of the Caddie and roared on down the highway toward the blinking neon sign on the outskirts of town that advertised, "Crossroads Bungalows. Weekly Rates Available."

Johnny sat waiting for him, lounging on a metal lawn chair under the overhanging porch of bungalow #3. He grinned languidly as Simon pulled up at the curb, and lifted his drink in salute.

"Hiya, Boss," Johnny said as Simon unfolded his six-foot frame and stepped out of the car. "Did you meet yourself coming in?"

Mountbank laughed and nodded. "A beautiful sight, Johnny, my boy—to see your own handsome face twenty feet high. Good job."

"There's one like it on every highway coming into town," Johnny said. "And we've advertised all the way over into South Dakota and down into Iowa. Radio, newspapers, flyers on every windshield within a sixty-mile radius. Should have no trouble filling the place."

"Fine, fine." Simon threw an arm around Johnny's shoulder and fingered the lapel of his light-blue western-style suit, tugging at the string tie playfully. "Looks like you're really getting into the spirit," he gibed. "Where'd you get these duds?"

"Gotta identify with the natives, Boss," Johnny said. He raised his left foot and pulled up the cuff of his pants to reveal an expensive gray snakeskin boot. "Hundred and forty bucks."

Simon let out a low whistle. "Hope we can afford it."

"After this gig, Boss, we'll be able to afford just about anything."

৯

Johnny Baptisto had earned his boots, Simon discovered. In addition to the ad campaign, Johnny had used his dark good looks and innocent schoolboy smile to worm his way into the confidence of almost every pastor in the area. By the time Simon hit town the day before the revival, forty-two ministers in the tri-county area had set their congregations to work planning pot-luck dinners, arranging for buses to bring people to the gym, offering pianos and organists and a mass choir from all the churches.

"There's gonna be so many saints there, we may not have room for the sinners," Johnny quipped as they drove across town to a pastors' reception at First Methodist.

"Well, then," Simon mused, "we'll just have to give the saints something to repent about."

The pastors' reception proved an enormous success. Simon Mountbank, in a fine gray suit that set off his salt-and-pepper hair, cut an imposing figure among the collection of weary-eyed, ordinary men and their mousy wives. Not a few among the clergy of

Angstrom County found themselves envying Mount-bank, wishing for a measure of his energy and flash. He drew them like moths to a flame, moving among them with charm and graciousness, making the men feel strong and spiritual and their wives lithe and beautiful.

"Reverend Mountbank," boomed Leon Sinclair, the rotund minister of First Methodist and spokesman for the group, "we all want you to know how grateful we are to God for sending you to minister to us." He raised a glass of pink punch in salute. "Many of our people have great needs—needs for healing and hope and heaven...." Everyone smiled at Sinclair's use of the advertising slogan, and he nodded in acknowledgment. "So, as we close this little gathering and prepare ourselves for the work ahead in the next two weeks, we'd like to pray for you, to commit you to our Lord, and to ask the Spirit to bless your efforts on His behalf."

The room buzzed for a moment or two as people scrambled to put down their punch glasses and gather around Mountbank. Simon knelt humbly, his head bowed, and the crowd circled around him. A dozen hands lighted on his shoulders and head, and silence descended upon the room. Here and there a murmured prayer went up, punctuated by whispered *amens.* When Sinclair finally closed with an impassioned plea for the Holy Spirit to take control, Simon raised his head to see tears in Sinclair's eyes.

"The man was actually *crying!*" Johnny said exultantly on the way back to the Crossroads Bungalows. "They're ready, Boss. This is gonna be a piece of cake."

ঝ

The first night of the Full Gospel Revival, Simon
Mountbank preached on sin. He was against it, he
said, and everyone laughed. Then he went on to
explain, in a passionate outburst of storytelling, how
he had seen a man come to a revival like this and
harden his heart to God. He left without giving his
life to Jesus, and met his doom that very night when
he ran head-on into a truck on a dark country road.
Mountbank described the scene of the accident in
terms that made the men cringe and the women hide
their faces in their hands. "None of us knows how
long we've got left," he finished. "The time to get
right with God is *now*. Now is the time for repentance; now is the day of salvation."

The singing was boisterous; the offering, moderate.
But when Mountbank gave the altar call, a man no
one in Turner's Crossroads had ever seen came forward, weeping profusely, stumbling down the center
aisle. "I been holding out on God!" the man wailed.
"He blessed me, but I didn't bless Him in return!" He
pulled a fistful of bills out of his pocket and stuffed
them into Mountbank's hand. "Take it, Preacher!" he
cried. "Use it for His glory. And let me give my life to
Jesus!"

While the stranger knelt before the makeshift stage
in the Crossroads gymnasium, Mountbank said quietly
into the microphone, "This brother has taught us a
valuable lesson tonight. God doesn't *need* our money
to accomplish His purposes, but He's promised to
bless us as we bless Him. You can't buy salvation; it's
a free gift. But you can demonstrate the reality of

your faith by giving to God's work."

The aisles began to fill as the organ strains of "Take My Life and Let It Be" echoed into the vaulted ceiling of the gym. *"Take my silver and my gold,"* Mountbank quoted as the music played behind him, *"Not a mite would I withhold.* There's a spirit of giving upon this place tonight, a spirit that says, *First I give my life to Jesus, then I give of my wealth to the Master.* Many of you want to do that; I can feel it. Come forward, if you feel that spirit upon you—God will bless your giving a hundredfold."

&

Whether God did it or not, the giving was blessed a hundredfold—or nearly, anyway. Simon and Johnny sat on the bed in Bungalow #3 and counted the take—just shy of twenty-one thousand for the first night.

"How many people did we have?" Simon asked.

"Twelve hundred."

"That's less than twenty bucks a head."

"It'll get better. We got two weeks to go. We can build slowly. And really, Boss, that's not bad for opening night."

"How much did you pay Lipkin?"

"Four hundred cash."

"Seems like a lot for one night's work, but I guess he's worth it."

"He's got his act down pat—very convincing."

"Where is he now?" Mountbank's brow furrowed.

"On his way back to Rapid City," Johnny said. "I

told him not to be seen within a hundred miles of here."

"What about the others?"

"Everybody's ready, Boss. We'll have a blind girl, age ten; a man with a club foot; and an old woman in a wheelchair, crippled by arthritis."

"What about the demoniac?" Mountbank said.

Johnny smiled, his even white teeth glinting in the light of the lamp. "I've got a real good one lined up, Boss. A woman who can go from hallucinations to sanity in two minutes flat."

"All right. Tell her she goes on Wednesday night during the sermon. We'll spread out the physical healings later on in the week."

By Thursday afternoon when the *Angstrom County Chronicle* came out, the news of Simon Mountbank's healing power was all over the county. The gymnasium was standing room only, and the revenues poured in like the spring runoff filling up the Blue River.

Johnny Baptisto had planned Friday night as the big show—the first of the physical healings. They'd start with the little blind girl, he thought, to get the sentimentality of the crowd aroused. After Wednesday night's deliverance of the schizophrenic woman in full view of twenty-five hundred observers, the place should be packed. It was a stroke of genius, having the woman interrupt the sermon with her hysterics. Now people didn't quite know what to expect, and they'd swallow almost anything.

ᐧᴥ

But Friday night's revival meeting took an

unanticipated turn. Just as Mountbank was finishing his sermon, entitled "I Am the God That Healeth Thee," a wizened old woman in a brown housedress and slippers limped down the aisle with a pale little boy in tow. The child's brown eyes widened with fear and wonder as they drew closer to the great evangelist. Simon shot a questioning look at Johnny, who raised his eyebrows and shrugged his shoulders. *I have no idea,* the gesture seemed to say.

"Reverend," the old woman said in a surprisingly strong voice, "my grandson Tucker here's got the bleedin' disease. Ever time he goes out and plays, he gets bruised and bleeds inside. It's killin' him. I want you to pray for him to be healed."

Mountbank raised his eyes from the old woman's face and looked out at the expectant crowd. *Now what?* Simon was accustomed to praying for invisible ailments: colds, rheumatism, emotional distress. But this was a different matter altogether.

Leon Sinclair got up from his chair and went over to where Simon stood on the platform. "This is Mrs. Aimee Sadler," he said softly. "She's lived on a farm out from town for fifty-five years."

"Sixty-one," Aimee corrected.

Sinclair smiled at her. "She's been a member of my church for—oh, thirty years."

"Forty-two," Aimee said.

"This boy is her daughter's child; she's been raising him since the girl left six years ago."

"Six and a half," Aimee said.

"Six and a half years ago," Sinclair conceded. "Anyway, Reverend Mountbank, the child is a hemophiliac.

The doctors say it's real bad; they're trying to control it, but it's getting worse."

Mountbank paused, then signaled to the old woman. "Bring the boy up here," he said. He turned to the crowd. "I want you all to pray," he instructed. "Sometimes God heals immediately, as He chose to do with the woman who received her deliverance on Wednesday night. Sometimes He heals gradually, over time." He paused and smiled to himself. It was a convenient out. "We don't know what He'll do here tonight, but Mrs. Sadler and her grandson are going to exercise their faith for his healing, and we're going to do the same."

A murmur ran through the audience. Nearly everybody in the auditorium knew Aimee Sadler. She couldn't read much, but she knew her Bible, and she had lived all her life in faith. It was a shame and a disgrace, the way her daughter had run off, leaving sixty-one-year-old Aimee saddled with a sick child. But Aimee had borne her cross with grace and good humor, and had brought little Tucker up in the fear of the Lord. He was the light of her life, the only family she had left, and everybody who knew and loved Aimee hurt with her.

Simon Mountbank eased the child into a folding chair and stood behind him, laying his big hands on the boy's shoulders. "Tucker," he said over the boy's head, "do you believe Jesus can heal you?" Tucker nodded solemnly, his face a pasty oval against the dark fabric of Mountbank's suit. "All right, then, we're going to pray, but you must have faith and not doubt, for he who doubtest is like a wave tossed by the wind."

It was another inspired moment. If the child went away unhealed, as he certainly would, the failure could be blamed on the subject's lack of faith rather than any deficiency in Mountbank's ministry.

So Mountbank prayed. He paced the length of the stage and back to little Tucker, who sat quietly in the chair, his feet swinging slightly. In the background, the organ played "Breathe on Me, Breath of God," and as Mountbank's prayer gained intensity, his voice nearly drowned out the music. At last he lighted upon Tucker with full force, pressing his head backward on his neck until the boy thought it would break. "Heal us, O Lord, and we shall be healed!" Mountbank shouted.

Without warning, something happened. "His face!" someone in the crowd shouted. "Look at his face!"

At first Simon thought they were talking about his own face; then he looked down at the boy. There was, perhaps, a change—a pink flush crept up his neck and into his cheeks. He smiled up at Simon. "Thank you, Sir," he said politely. "I feel much better now."

Aimee Sadler stood at the foot of the steps leading up to the platform, tears streaming down her wrinkled cheeks. She looked not at her little grandson, who ran across the stage toward the steps, but heavenward, her lips moving in silent thanksgiving.

The noise of the crowd, which had been steadily increasing in volume, quieted suddenly in a collective gasp. Tucker, on his way back to his grandmother, tripped at the top of the stairs and hurtled headlong down the four steps. His head crashed against the iron handrail, and he lay motionless at the bottom, blood pulsing from a shallow gash over his right eye.

"Call a doctor!" someone yelled. "Is there a doctor here?"

Tucker stirred, then sat up awkwardly. "No," he murmured weakly, pressing a hand to his bleeding head. "I—I'm all right."

Aimee gathered the boy into her arms and held him, rocking him softly and crying, "Jesus, Jesus," as her tears mingled with the blood on his forehead. She reached a withered hand to brush back the hair matted in the wound, then stopped, her hand trembling in mid-air. "It's clotting," she whispered. Then louder, "It's clotting! Praise Jesus, he's healed!"

⁂

The Friday night revenues totaled nearly forty-seven thousand dollars. Johnny Baptisto counted out the take, stacking the bills neatly in piles of a thousand on the foot of the bed.

"This is great, Boss!" he said. "At this rate, by the time the revival is over, we'll—"

"The revival *is* over," Simon Mountbank said, his voice a low monotone. "I'm done."

"What are you talking about, Boss?" Johnny demanded. "We're just getting started. After what happened tonight—"

"And just what *did* happen tonight?" Simon demanded, sitting up suddenly and knocking several of the piles of bills onto the floor.

Johnny bent over and gathered up the loot. He looked over his shoulder at Mountbank. "A hemophiliac kid got healed, to all appearances."

"Exactly. And how, precisely, did this healing take place?"

Johnny shrugged, then cracked his most charming schoolboy grin. "He was prayed for by a great faith healer," he said with just a touch of sarcasm in his tone. "So what?"

"So we both know I had nothing to do with what happened back there—" Mountbank lay down again and stared at the water-stained ceiling, a haunted, empty expression filling his eyes.

"Yeah. So?" Johnny obviously didn't understand what was eating at Simon.

"Johnny," Simon said wearily, "if that boy's healing wasn't a set-up like all the physical healings we've pulled off in the past, if I didn't plan it, then who did?"

"I dunno. God, maybe?"

"God." Simon spoke the word carefully, quietly, with no hint of either the private cynicism or the public oratory that usually accompanied his utterance of the name.

Even Johnny, who normally overlooked the significant little nuances, couldn't miss the difference in Simon's tone.

"C'mon, Boss, you don't really believe—"

"I don't know what I believe," Simon whispered. "But I do know we're done. Finished."

Johnny shook his head. "Boss, the way I see it, it doesn't *matter* what happened to that kid tonight. We're on a roll, and if we give it up now—"

"We're giving it up," Simon said. "Now, tonight. Take your cut, pay off your actors."

"They haven't done anything yet," Johnny protested.

"Pay them off anyway. Fulfill your contracts. Pay everybody we owe, and keep your percentage. Then check out of this hotel and get on the road."

"But, Boss—"

Simon looked directly into Johnny's dark eyes, and Johnny saw there an expression he had never seen before—an uncertainty, an indecision. "I'm sorry, Johnny. I really am. You are good, really good, at what you do. I'll miss you. But this is where our paths part."

Johnny Baptisto shook his head sadly. Without a word, he counted out his share of the money and separated what he owed to the actors and the radio station. He left the rest—nearly thirty thousand—in a bag on the table. When he closed the door behind him, Simon Mountbank still lay on the bed, staring vacantly at the water stain on the ceiling.

❧

The Full Gospel Revival went on without Simon Mountbank. Leon Sinclair took over, explaining that Reverend Mountbank had been stricken with heart trouble and could not complete the week of meetings. A few left, disgruntled that the star of the show had failed to appear. But most stayed, and the Crossroads High School gymnasium, although not crowded to capacity, seemed full enough.

A few more healings occurred as the faithful prayed for the sick. Young Tucker gave a timid testimony of his own healing, and his grandmother Aimee sat up front to counsel with those who came to give their lives to Jesus. In all, about seven hundred souls were ushered into the Kingdom during the last week of the Revival, and some twelve hundred others from the sponsoring churches found a new enthusiasm for things spiritual.

ॐ

On the final night of the Revival, the call went out for the faithful to take the Word back to their churches and communities, to live out the truth of God's love among their neighbors. Caught up in worship, no one noticed as a man in blue jeans and a rumpled gray windbreaker, with salt-and-pepper hair and a week's stubble of gray beard, knelt on the varnished floor in the back of the gymnasium and gave his heart to God.

When the treasurer from First Methodist sorted through the offering for the last night, he found a tan canvas bag containing nearly sixty thousand dollars in cash. Wrapped around one stack of bills was a page torn from the hymnal they'd used for the Revival. Highlighted with a yellow marker, the words jumped off the page:

TAKE MY SILVER AND MY GOLD,
NOT A MITE WOULD I WITHHOLD....

No one knew where the money had come from. But when Leon Sinclair closed the final prayer meeting of the area pastors, he interceded fervently for Simon Mountbank, thanking God for his ministry. "Give him strength to serve Thee, dear Lord," Sinclair prayed, "and heal his heart, O God."

ॐ

Critical Choice

**Choose for yourselves this day
whom you will serve...."
—Joshua 24:15**

RUBY BRUSHED away the tears that threatened to fall and turned back to the bedside where her father lay dying. "Do you understand what I've told you, honey?" he gasped, fighting for breath.

"Yes, Daddy." Ruby sighed. "You want me to take care of Mama just like you did."

"You've always been a good girl," the dying man wheezed. "You've always done what Daddy told you, and I know you'll keep on being a good girl after I'm gone—"

"Daddy, don't!" Ruby still fought against the rising tears, but weariness was beginning to replace grief.

She just wanted to go home and go to bed.

"The will's all set," he continued, the rasp in his voice growing louder. "You and your mama will be well provided for, but Mama will need you even more now—" The long speech winded him, and his words dissolved in a spasm of weak coughing.

Mama needs me, all right. Ruby was ashamed of the thought the moment it occurred to her, but she was too exhausted to stem the tide of cynicism that rose to the surface. *Mama doesn't drive, or write checks, or take care of the house. She's had a cook for the last twenty years, and I doubt if she's ever cleaned a toilet in her whole precious, protected life—*

"Ruby—" her father's voice cut into her thoughts, and she felt caught, the way she had years ago when he had found her private diary and read in her little-girl scrawl, *I hate Mama.* She had no way of knowing that most little girls think the same things and go through the same struggles. And Daddy didn't tell her. But from then on she carefully guarded her thoughts and learned, over the years, how to please Mama and keep Daddy happy.

"Ruby—" he said again, reaching a shaking hand toward her. "You are my jewel, and Mama is my treasure. Take care of her for me...."

"Yes, Daddy, I will."

He gripped her hand, and his strength surprised her. "Promise!" he whispered fiercely, his fingernails cutting tiny crescents into the top of her hand. "Promise you will do as I ask; swear it on the honor of my memory!"

Ruby's throat went dry, and a shiver ran down her

neck. She had never seen her father like this before. This man was not the Daddy she had known for twenty-six years, and he frightened her. But she couldn't break and run away, no matter how much she wanted to. "I promise," Ruby whispered, her tears breaking at last. "I promise, Daddy."

He squeezed her hand feebly and exhaled a final rattling breath, thick with the scent of death, into his daughter's nostrils.

⋆

The week after the funeral, Ruby escorted Mama into the lawyer's office to hear the reading of Daddy's will. The estate was sizeable; she and her mother would never want for anything money could buy. Everything, of course, went to Mama and Ruby. "With one contingency," the lawyer read, his face expressionless. "My daughter, Ruby Childress Lawfort, shall serve as executrix of the estate. In order to be granted her individual interest in the estate, she shall not marry or move from the house of her mother, as long as her mother shall live."

Ruby drew in a breath. *So that's what he meant by "taking care of Mama"!* The lawyer continued, unperturbed. "Should my daughter choose to marry or move from the family home during the remainder of her mother's natural life, her portion of this estate shall revert to her mother, and the entire estate, at her mother's death, shall be divided among the charitable institutions specified below...."

Ruby's mind reeled. She had every intention of seeing to it that Mama was cared for, of course, even though she disagreed with Daddy over the way he spoiled and pampered Mama. Now he had made sure she would do it—and do it his way!

࿐

Ruby slammed the car into park, stepped out, and headed for the side door of St. Stephen's. *Mama will be waiting,* she thought, *and I have to be at the farm in forty-five minutes.* She muttered a disgusted curse under her breath and pulled the door open.

The tiled halls of St. Stephen's Nursing Home smelled faintly of antiseptic and urine. As she passed open doors on the way to Mama's room, Ruby heard the familiar sounds of age fighting every step of the way toward eternity.

"Arnold?" Bessie Markham in 213 whined. "Is that you, Arnold?"

"Arnold died the year after Daddy," Ruby murmured to nobody in particular as she passed by. "Twenty years ago. Twenty years."

Elizabeth Skogen, one of the day nurses, met Ruby as she rounded the corner. "Say, Ruby, that's a lovely outfit," Liz said. "You seem to be looking younger every year."

Ruby smiled self-consciously. At 46, she could, indeed, have passed for ten years younger. In the past two years she had taken off fifty-two pounds, adopted a new hairstyle, and renovated her wardrobe. Now she walked three miles a day. And Liz was right—she did look terrific. Her new charcoal wool blazer set off the mauve silk blouse and gray slacks, complementing her graying hair perfectly. *Just the kind of classic casual look Justin likes*, thought Ruby; then, as if her thoughts might give her away, she asked quickly, "Where's Mama?"

"On the sunporch," Liz replied, motioning down the hall.

№

Through the French doors leading to the sunporch, Ruby could see the tiny, hunched figure of her mother slumping in a wheelchair.

"Now, Miss Muriel, don't we want to eat our prunes today?" a jovial black aide was entreating as Ruby entered. She held out a small bowl of brown mash and smiled broadly at Ruby.

"Miss Ruby, your Mama she just don't want to cooperate."

"That's OK, Lettie," Ruby responded, taking the bowl and grimacing at its contents. "Can't say as I blame her, but I'll try to get her to eat it."

"Thanks, Miss Ruby. I'll be on my way, then." Lettie beat a hasty retreat into the hall.

Ruby walked around to the front of the wheelchair. Her mother's thinning white hair moved gently in the breeze as her head bobbed in an uncertain rhythm. "Mama?" Ruby said quietly, kissing her mother's wrinkled velvet cheek and then kneeling down in front of the wheelchair. "Mama? You need to eat your prunes, now—"

Mama's head came up slowly, her watery blue eyes squinting as she peered into the face before her. "I don't know you!" she shrieked suddenly. "You get outta here!"

"Mama, it's Ruby. Your daughter. I come to see you every day. You remember."

"Roooody?" the old woman howled. "Roooody's dead, fool! Been dead for a hundred years!"

"Not Rudy, Mama," persisted the daughter, wondering who Rudy was. *"Ruby."*

"Hee, hee, hee," Mama cackled. "Rooooby—rooooby. Rooooby's a jewel, everybody knows that. And you ain't no jewel!" She paused. "Except maybe for this—" She fingered the front of Ruby's silk blouse, popping off the center button as she pulled.

"Mama, why don't you try to eat?" Ruby tried another tack, settling down in the chair beside her mother and offering her a spoonful of the prunes.

"Killerrr," the woman growled savagely. "Everybody's trying to kill me, to poison me. Murderer!" She slapped the bowl of prunes away with surprising force, flinging the brown mush across the sleeve of Ruby's new blazer.

"Mama!" Ruby began, but she knew a reprimand would do no good. It had been the same for weeks now—her mother, still physically strong at eighty-four, was quickly losing touch with reality. The doctors could do nothing but care for her body—as the staff of St. Stephen's was doing with remarkable patience and efficiency. She might live another fifteen years. But her mind was going—she rarely recognized Ruby anymore, and she was becoming increasingly hostile and difficult to handle.

Ruby wiped the prunes off her sleeve with a tissue, kissed her mother quickly, and headed toward the door. "See you tomorrow, Mama," she whispered, swallowing the lump that rose in her throat.

❧

Following the gravel road out of town toward Justin's farm, Ruby opened the car window and let the chilly, early-spring breeze blow through. If anything could restore her sagging spirits, it was a drive in the country and the prospect of an evening with Justin.

She followed the familiar roads, bordered on each side by plowed fields, black and rich, awaiting spring planting. When the road veered north, she slowed down and turned west into the farm road beside the mailbox marked "J. Harte."

In the two years since she had met Justin, Ruby had never tired of the beauty of this drive up to Justin's home. The private road wound two miles back into the woods, a broad serpentine path covered by the arch of tree limbs. At last the road broke into a clearing on the hill where the old Harte homestead stood—a large, sturdy farmhouse, light gray in color, with a wraparound porch on three sides facing the woods and a huge enclosed porch on the back. From this back porch, Justin had the best vantage point in the county—open hills breaking away toward the river in the distance, and a perfect view of any available sunset.

There is simply no comparison, Ruby had told Justin the first time she came to the farm, *between this and our house in town.* Although the Harte place was modest, it was warm and comfortable and inviting. The Lawfort House, ostentatious in its abundance, was the biggest, richest, finest house in Turner's Crossroads.

One block off Main Street, the Lawfort House was a source of both pride and envy for the community. But since her father's death twenty years before—even, if she were honest, long before he died—that house had become a prison for her; an opulent showplace of a cell, to be sure, but a place of solitary confinement nevertheless.

But that was before Justin.

❧

As Ruby drove up, the front door opened and Justin emerged, grinning broadly. Dressed in jeans and a burgundy sweater, he stood on the porch leaning against a post. His dark hair and beard were flecked with gray, and his brown eyes gleamed as he watched her come up the walk. When she reached the top step, he threw his arms around her and laughed gently into her ear. "Hello, Sweetheart; I thought you'd never make it." Then he kissed her—that tender, lingering kiss that always took her breath away—and stepped back.

"Any trouble?" His eyes took in the torn blouse.

"Just Mama," Ruby sighed. "She's getting worse and worse."

"You want to tell me about it?"

"There's not much to tell. She didn't recognize me again today, and she baptized me in mashed prunes."

"I could tell." He wrinkled his nose and reached for her hand. "Come on; we'll get the prunes out, and then we'll talk. I've got chicken on the grill and cheesecake cooling in the fridge."

"What's the occasion?" Ruby murmured, intrigued.

"Just your being here, Love," he whispered. Then he kissed her again and led her into the house.

They ate their dinner at the small round breakfast table in the corner of the porch, at first bathed in the orange and pink glow of a radiant sunset, then later drawn together over the pale flicker of a single candle.

"Let's have coffee in the den," Justin suggested, taking the candle in one hand and the coffee pot in the other. "It's still cool enough for a fire, and I've already laid the logs in the fireplace."

When the coffee was finished, the candle burned low, and the conversation about the day's events drawn to a close, Justin reached into the coffee table drawer and drew out a small box.

"Ruby," he said intently, his eyes never leaving hers, "we need to talk—really talk." He opened the box and placed it in her palm. There, in the warm light of the fire, glowed a small diamond solitaire.

"Marry me, Ruby," he said simply. "Marry me now."

"Oh, Justin," Ruby sighed, "we've been through this all before. You know my situation. I love you, and I want to be with you, but I can't marry you. Not now, anyway."

Justin stood up, took her hands, and pulled her from the floor in front of the fireplace up onto the couch. He reached behind her head and snapped on a lamp.

"Ruby," he insisted, putting a hand under her chin and turning her face toward him, "the money isn't that important. We can be very comfortable here, and—"

"Don't you think I've thought of all that?" She snapped the box shut and handed it back to him. "But think practically, Justin. Times are tough. The farming economy's bottoming out, and my inheritance money could be a great boon to us. You could expand, buy more stock, hire some help—"

"Ruby, you know I'm no farmer. Except for this tract of woodland, all the crop land I own is rented out, being worked by others. I want to write music, and I can do it, here, in this place of peace and solitude."

Ruby started to respond, then closed her mouth, took a deep breath, and waited for a moment. When she did speak, her voice was controlled and gentle. "Yes, Justin, and your music is beautiful. That inheritance could give you the freedom to spend time on it. All the more reason we should wait."

"Wait for what?" Justin asked quietly. "For your mother's death?"

The impact of the words slapped Ruby into realization. "Yes," she said finally. "I guess that is what we're waiting for. Waiting for Mama to die."

"But we don't need to wait, Sweetheart. We don't need the big showy house in town. We don't need your daddy's money. We need each other."

Ruby put her arms around Justin and laid her head on his shoulder. "There's more to it than the money, Justin."

"Meaning?"

"My promise to Daddy. I told him I'd take care of Mama. And he'd just die if he knew—"

Justin squeezed her quickly and they both laughed at her slip of the tongue.

"Well, you know what I mean," she continued. "I promised."

"And he laid down the terms of the promise in his will," Justin said, tensing with anger. "He had no right to lay that kind of burden on you, no right to extract such a promise from his only daughter. He was determined to control you as he always had, even twenty years after his death!"

"Daddy was forty when I was born," Ruby mused. "Mama was thirty-eight. The doctors said they should never have had a child so late in life; Mama was so frail from the time I was born—"

"Mama was pampered from before the time you were born," corrected Justin gently.

"True. And there were times I hated them both for it. But I did promise Daddy—"

"Ruby, a promise should be an expression of joyful commitment, not a chain to bind you to someone else's desires. The promise you made to your father on his deathbed was wrong—for both of you. He forced it upon you, but you don't have to live with that control for the rest of your life."

Ruby slid out of Justin's arms and moved over to the fireplace. She stirred the coals thoughtfully, then placed two more logs on the grate.

"I've never broken my word to them," she said. "I've always done what was expected."

"Ruby, do you love me?"

"Of course I do!" Tears rose to Ruby's eyes and glinted in the light of the rising flame.

"In two months I'll be fifty years old," Justin murmured. "You're forty-six. We deserve to be happy, to have the chance to grow old together."

Ruby knew he was right. She had been over this in

her mind a thousand times. She wanted to marry him, but somehow she couldn't let go of the security she had. They needed that inheritance money, she reasoned. Things would be so much easier for them if....

She took a deep breath and said the words she had rehearsed over and over again. "We could just live together," she said in a wavering voice. "I could keep the house in town; nobody would have to know—Mama certainly wouldn't understand...." Her voice trailed off. He would never buy it, and she didn't really mean it. It was a suggestion born out of desperation.

He smiled grimly, knowing that it wasn't a viable option, knowing that she didn't really want it that way. "First, you know people would find out—in a town this size, it's inevitable. More importantly, I absolutely refuse to have you under those conditions. In the two years since I moved back to town, we've been happy together; we've learned to love each other. I want to *marry* you, not just make love to you. I want you to choose commitment to me."

His last words stung more sharply than he had intended. They pierced an old wound in her, deep in a secret, hidden chamber. She would have to risk everything, to give up the known for the unknown, to abandon the security of her inheritance, in order to have Justin. "I'd better go," she said, snatching her blazer from the coat rack in the corner. "I'll call you tomorrow, Justin." She kissed him briefly and was out the door before he could get to his feet.

"I love you, Ruby!" he shouted as she gunned the engine. She drove away, leaving a cloud of dust floating in the moonlight.

&

"I hoped you'd get here in time!" Dr. Wilson's voice was edged with panic as he led Ruby down the hospital hall toward her mother's room. "When they called from St. Stephen's, I came right away. But there wasn't much I could do."

Ruby held her breath as she entered the intensive care facility. On the bed before her, obscured by tubes and surrounded by machines, lay the tiny, wrinkled form of her mother. "She apparently had a stroke in her room," the doctor continued. "It was a few minutes before anyone found her. By that time she had sustained significant brain damage."

"When did it happen?"

"Around seven. The nurses tried to call, but they couldn't reach you."

"I was out to dinner." Ruby looked at her watch. Eleven-thirty p.m. She had arrived home from Justin's at ten-fifteen to find a note from the housekeeper. *CALL ST. STEPHEN'S IMMEDIATELY. EMERGENCY.* Dr. Wilson had waited at the hospital until Ruby arrived.

"What happens now?" Ruby was trying to keep her mind focused on the situation at hand, but she kept remembering her father and thinking about Justin.

"We don't know. The life support systems could keep her alive like this for months—maybe years. Or she could develop complications before the night is out. Or we could decide—"

"To pull the plug?" In her mind's eye Ruby saw a flash of Justin's face and heard the words again: *We're waiting for Mama to die.*

Ruby walked to the bed and picked up her mother's hand. The skin was dry and cool, like fine parchment, spotted with age, the veins bulging. She stroked the hand absently, whispering, "Good-bye, Mama. I do love you, although I was angry—so angry—at the way Daddy kept you dependent on him. Soon you'll be free, Mama. Free of the pain; free of your dependency on other people. And I can be free, too. I can make the choice I should have made a long time ago."

Ruby gently laid the hand back on the bed and turned to the doctor. "No," she heard herself saying, as if she were eavesdropping on someone else's conversation. "No, we won't make that decision yet. Do everything you can for her, Dr. Wilson. I'll be in touch."

❧

The next morning Ruby went to see her father's lawyer. "Mr. Dillon," she said, settling herself on the chair opposite the attorney's desk, "I've come to talk about my father's will."

"Yes, Miss Lawfort. I must say I was somewhat taken aback by the terms of that particular will. Your father must have loved your mother very much, and known you would be willing and able to care for her as you have over the years. Quite remarkable, if I do say—"

"Mr. Dillon," Ruby interrupted, "I'm afraid I don't have time for all this. I've made a decision that you need to act upon immediately. I'm getting married—as soon as possible. Beginning today, I want you to take whatever steps are necessary to enforce the terms of my father's will and begin plans for distributing his money to the charities he specified."

"But Miss Lawfort!" Dillon protested. "It's been so many years, and your mother is now—well, not young. Don't you think you might reconsider? After all, we are talking about a substantial sum of money— by this time close to a million dollars, I believe."

Ruby gasped audibly. She knew her father was well off, but she had no idea of the total dollar amount of the estate. *We would be set for life!* she thought briefly. Then, resolutely, she said, "It's a matter of principle, Mr. Dillon, not time or money."

"Very well, Miss Lawfort." He pulled a paper out of the file before him. "It's all been prepared in the event of such a decision. You need to sign here, and here—" he pointed. "But once you have signed this document, it cannot be rescinded. You voluntarily abandon all rights to this estate, and your portion of the inheritance reverts to your mother. At the time of her death, the disbursement of funds will commence."

Ruby hesitated, her pen poised over the document. "For you, Justin," she murmured under her breath. "For us." Then she signed her name quickly, turned on her heel, and left the office.

❧

Two days later, Mama died. Her kidneys failed, and she slipped into eternity without ever regaining consciousness.

Justin stood with his arm around Ruby as the townspeople came and went from the funeral home.

The nurses from St. Stephen's came to express their regrets and stayed to exclaim over Ruby's engagement ring.

"It's kinda bad timing for such a joyous occasion," commented Lettie with a sad smile.

"Any regrets?" asked Justin when the women were gone.

"Two," replied Ruby immediately. "First, waiting so long to make this decision." She fingered the ring lovingly. "I've never felt so free in my life."

"And second?"

"The money, Justin. I'm sorry—I still feel that things would be a lot easier for us if I hadn't given it up."

"Then why did you? You knew your mother could go at any time—you could have waited, and had me and the money both."

"Not really. Not the way I wanted it, anyway. I had to make a decision, to choose to commit myself to you, not let circumstances decide for me."

Justin bent forward and put his arms around Ruby. But just as he was about to kiss her, he heard a commotion behind them.

"Ahem! Ah, well, Miss Lawfort—" Dillon, obviously flustered by this unseemly demonstration of affection in the hall of the funeral home, shifted from one foot to the other. "I—I just wanted to express my sympathy, Miss Lawfort; and my congratulations, too. Although I must say I wish you had decided to wait just a bit longer. As circumstances turned out, the timing of your decision was, well—unfortunate."

"Circumstances turned out just fine, Mr. Dillon."

Ruby squeezed Justin's hand. "And the timing was quite fortunate." Then she saw a movement in the adjoining room. Murmuring, "Will you gentlemen excuse me? I see a friend I need to speak to," she slipped from Justin's side and was gone.

Harrumphing and shifting, Dillon stood there, pained, until Justin rescued him. "Mr.—uh, Dillon, is it? Please forgive my fiancée for not introducing us. She's been under a lot of stress lately. I'm Justin Harte."

"*The* Justin Harte?" the lawyer asked incredulously. "Why, sir, this *is* a pleasure! Lawrence Dillon, Miss Lawfort's attorney—" Dillon pumped Justin's arm vigorously. "I've wanted to meet you for a long time," he said. "But you have a reputation for being rather a hermit."

"I value my privacy, so I try to keep out of the public eye," Justin answered simply.

"I've heard," Dillon went on, "that Harteland Enterprises owns just about half the land in this county—including the land under the new interstate, the power company right-of-way, and a few miscellaneous oil fields in Oklahoma, if I have my facts correct."

Justin nodded in silent acknowledgment.

"Well, that girl's no fool, I can say that for her," Dillon declared. "Why, if half what I've heard is true, Harteland is easily worth ten times what her old man left her."

Justin smiled wryly. "It is," he said quietly, "but she doesn't know that."

Dillon gaped at Justin. "She doesn't *know?*"

"Not yet," he answered. "There will be plenty of

time—a whole lifetime—for her to discover her new inheritance."

Justin's countenance lit up as Ruby made her way back through the crowd toward her fiancé and her lawyer.

"Well, well, Miss Lawfort!" Dillon chuckled, smiling conspiratorily at Ruby. "I've been having a most interesting conversation with your Mr. Harte. Now I understand why you weren't concerned about letting go of your father's inheritance. You've got yourself quite a prize there!" He winked broadly at Justin.

She stared blankly, first at Dillon, then at Justin. "I'm not quite sure what you mean, Mr. Dillon," Ruby said. "But as I said before, I have no regrets. I should have made this decision long ago. I may have given up a sizeable inheritance, Mr. Dillon, but I got Justin in the bargain. And he is, indeed, a treasure to me."

☙

Rapture Piggot and the Fighting Nun

Lord, do you want us to call down
fire from heaven to destroy them?"
—Luke 9:54

MAVIS KITCHENS, wiping down the counter at the Four Korners Kafe, was the first to see Rapture Pigott standing in the doorway. She ducked her head and scrubbed viciously at a spot of dried pancake syrup, hoping to avoid his eyes.

No one else in the cafe had seen him enter. In the far corner booth, the rattle and slap of the dice cup on the Formica tabletop was greeted with a roar of approval as Eddie Bjerke lost the round to Marvin Angstrom. For the third time this week, Eddie had to buy coffee for the guys. From every other table, animated conversations surged upward and converged in one great rumble of community goodwill. The Four Korners at 10 a.m. was a noisy, happy, relaxed place.

Then someone caught wind of Rapture Pigott's presence—not a difficult matter, since he worked at the stockyards and never thought to change his boots before coming into town. No one looked up, but a mysterious quieting force made its way around the room in a slow half-circle. Chairs scraped on the linoleum as people adjusted their seats and turned their backs toward the door. Conversations dropped into silence, then resumed in a low murmur around each table.

No one dared to meet Rapture Pigott's smiling gaze; the slightest sign of recognition could be taken for invitation, and nearly everyone in Turner's Crossroads knew what could happen if Rapture got started.

Everyone, that is, except Sister Gertrude Hoffstadt.

&

Sister Gertrude sat alone at a small table near the window, flipping through a sheaf of yellow legal-pad pages. Her unopened mail lay on the table next to her coffee cup. She had spent the morning with the park director, making plans for the annual St. Sebaldus Memorial Day Family Picnic, setting up volleyball nets and arranging picnic tables in Blue River Park.

Dressed in jeans and a faded Notre Dame sweatshirt, she hardly looked the part of a nun, except for the tiny silver crucifix that hung around her neck on a slender silver chain.

When Rapture Pigott entered the cafe, Sister Gertrude did the unthinkable. She looked up, adjusted her round gold-rimmed glasses, and smiled.

>◆

Rapture stood for a moment with the door open behind him, wiping the manure from his boots on the mat. Every table was occupied, every chair filled, every back turned toward him, every head down in conversation. This was not going to be easy.

Then he spotted her, at the table next to the window—a lone middle-aged woman, rather thin and pale, looking up at him with startling blue eyes, smiling.

Rapture removed his seed-corn cap and ran a hand through his thinning hair. Cap in hand, he moved toward the woman's table and stood there for a moment, beaming down at her.

"Excuse me, ma'am," he said politely. "Would you mind if I shared your table? There don't seem to be anyplace else to sit."

>◆

Sister Gertrude's placid gaze took him in from the ground up: mucky boots, overalls with streaks of mud on the cuffs, a blue denim work shirt, an advertising jacket for a seed company—a different company than the one on his cap. The man's face was round and ruddy, a stark contrast to his white hair. His eyes crinkled around the corners, and his broad smile showed a gleam of gold behind one front tooth. True, he did emanate the scent known locally as *Eau d'Feed Lot,* but so did most of the farmers who came into town for supplies and stayed for coffee at the Four

Korners. A harmless enough sort, Gertrude thought.

"Certainly," she said at last. "Do sit down."

The man sat, placing his stained cap carefully on top of the napkin dispenser. Mavis Kitchens appeared with a cup of coffee and set it down next to his elbow without a word. She refilled Sister Gertrude's cup and turned away.

"Thanks, Mavis," he said, a little too loud. "God bless you."

Mavis grunted and moved back behind the counter.

The man turned on Gertrude, his round face beaming. "Name's Lawrence Pigott," he said, extending a rough, stained hand and shaking hers enthusiastically. "But folks around here call me Rapture. Bet you can't guess why."

Gertrude opened her mouth to reply, but he went on without waiting for an answer. "'Cause I'm ready for the Rapture!" he said, laughing heartily. "I'm waiting for my Jesus to return, and when He does— whoosh!—I'm gonna be caught up together with Him in the clouds, to meet the Lord in the air!"

Over his shoulder, Gertrude caught a glimpse of a few faces turned their way. Several eyebrows lifted, and a couple of heads shook before turning away again.

Rapture Pigott took a long swallow of coffee, choking a little as he set the cup down. "Hot!" he sputtered, then he grinned again. "But not near as hot as it's gonna be someday for those who don't repent!"

He fished into his shirt pocket and came out with a rumpled booklet, stained with dirty fingerprints and soft from handling.

THE WAY TO EVERLASTING PEACE, it said in bold black letters across a bright yellow background. He shoved it in her direction.

"I didn't catch your name, Sister," he said suddenly, piercing her with an intense look.

Sister Gertrude's head jerked up. *Does he know who I am?* she wondered briefly. Then she caught a glimpse of Mavis Kitchens behind the cash register, her shoulders shaking with silent laughter. Gertrude smiled to herself. He didn't know; apparently there was a lot he didn't know.

"Gertrude Hoffstadt," she answered.

"You must be new in town," he said. "Haven't seen you around much."

"Ah...yes," she said finally. "I've only been here a short time."

He stared at the plain gold band on her finger. "Hoffstadt...Hoffstadt," he repeated, squinting at the ceiling. "Don't believe I know your husband, ma'am. Does he work around here?"

Sister Gertrude suppressed a laugh. "Sometimes," she said. "When he can."

A puzzled expression flashed over Rapture Pigott's countenance. "Oh. Well, what line of work is he in?"

"Sheep," Sister Gertrude replied.

Rapture's face lit up in an expression of delight. "A sheep farmer? Yeah, I remember—down south of town; that must be your place. Well, you tell your husband that when he's ready to slaughter, to bring 'em to me over at Svenson's Stockyards. I'll see to it that he gets a good price—"

Sister Gertrude slanted a look at Rapture. "We don't

slaughter our sheep," she said quietly.

"Ah," Rapture said, "you raise 'em for wool. Good market in wool nowadays."

Sister Gertrude started to reply, but was interrupted as Mavis Kitchens appeared to refill their coffee cups. She had a wide smile on her face, and she winked at Sister Gertrude when Rapture wasn't looking. "You need anything else?"

"No, thank you," Gertrude said. "We're doing just fine."

"I can see that," Mavis said. "Holler if you need any help."

When Mavis was gone, Rapture leaned forward and said secretively, "You're wrong, you know."

"About what?" Sister Gertrude whispered.

"About not needing anything else." He narrowed his eyes and peered at her. "I couldn't help noticing that cross you're wearing—"

Gertrude fingered the crucifix tenderly. "And?"

"Well, I gotta tell you, Sister, that cross is a blasphemy against the truth of God's Word."

She sank back in her chair. "I beg your pardon?"

"You see," he said, leaning forward again, his voice gaining volume. "That cross shows Jesus still hanging up there, dead. But the Bible says that Jesus hath been resurrected on the third day. He's not dead; He's alive, hallelujah!"

With the closing *hallelujah*, Rapture Pigott stamped his foot, scattering dried manure in a half-circle around his boot. From behind the counter, Mavis Kitchens glared at him.

He stared intently at the crucifix. "Where did you

come by that thing, anyway?"

"It belonged to my grandmother—"

"You got Catholic blood in your background?" he interrupted. "Let me tell you, Sister; you need to hear the True Word of God, the unadulterated gospel, in order to be saved."

Sister Gertrude raised her eyebrows. "Really?" she said, with an edge in her tone.

"Really," he said earnestly.

"I happen to know a number of Catholics who might disagree with you," she said, her words clipped. "Catholics who are completely devoted to Christ."

"I'm not saying, mind you, that Catholics can't get the true faith," Rapture protested. "Maybe they can, by the Grace of God and the Power of the Blood. Maybe your grandmother, God bless her, was a true Christian. But I can't figure that any true Christian would *stay* in a church tainted by idolatry."

Sister Gertrude fought against the rising tide of anger that threatened to engulf her. Even as a child she had been a fighter, one who, in her mother's words, "did not bear fools gladly." She entertained a fleeting mental image of bloodying the Raptured One's nose and wiping her hands on the front of her Notre Dame shirt.

But her years as a nun had taught her to be a peacemaker—at least on the outside. And most of the time she managed to keep her temper under control.

She clenched her fists under the table and asked, "And what church do you attend, Mr. Pigott?"

He grinned. "I," he said proudly, "am a member of the First Freewill Holiness Church." He laughed and pounded on the table, rattling the coffee cups. "I'm FIRST in God's heart; I'm FREE by His grace; I'm walking in His WILL, and I'm surrendered to the call to HOLINESS! Praise God!"

He pushed the tattered tract across the table toward her. "I'd like to share with you something that I've found very helpful," he said. "This little booklet outlines four simple steps to getting saved—it'll get you headed for heaven in no time."

He opened the tract and read, following the words with a grimy forefinger. "First, you gotta ADMIT that you're a sinner. Do you know that you're a sinner, Sister?"

Sister Gertrude resisted the impulse to laugh out loud. Her thoughts about this man, certainly, would qualify her for a rather lengthy confession. "Mmmm," she murmured.

"Fine, fine," he said, pressing on. "Now you gotta BELIEVE that Jesus died for your sins." He paused, looking at the crucifix she wore. "And that He was resurrected, so He isn't dead any more," he added hurriedly.

"Mmmm-hmmm," she said.

"OK, then you need to CONFESS your faith in Him, and last, DENY thyself, take up thy cross, and follow after Him. It's as simple as A,B,C. And D, of course."

Sister Gertrude stared blankly at him, saying nothing, giving nothing away. Suddenly she realized that the entire cafe had grown deadly quiet. Everyone sat watching, listening, waiting to hear her response.

"Have you ever taken these important steps to salvation?" Rapture Pigott recited, his voice insistent.

She shook her head, pushing down the caustic, unchristian responses that rose to the surface of her mind. A nun could not say such things...should not even *think* them. But, then, Sister Gertrude had always had problems with uncontrollable thoughts about such people. She could at least keep them to herself.

He interpreted her silence as the response he was looking for. "Have you ever been baptized, Sister?" he asked.

She gaped at him. "Well, yes," she stammered.

"No, I mean *really* baptized. Getting sprinkled as a baby doesn't count, you know."

"Is that so?"

"Yes, that's so. *Real* baptism, in the Bible sense, is like John the Baptizer did it in the Jordan River. Believer's baptism, all the way under."

They obviously held you under a little too long, Sister Gertrude thought. But she said nothing.

"Well, listen," Rapture said. "I'll tell you what we'll do. Our church is having a baptism service on Memorial Day out at the Blue River Park swimming beach. You pray with me now and accept Jesus into your heart. Then I'll arrange it with my pastor to baptize you along with the others at our service."

An image presented itself, fully formed, in Sister Gertrude's mind—the entire parish of St. Sebaldus standing on the riverbank, hot dogs in hand, to see their nun being immersed in the murky waters of the Blue River.

Suddenly an idea struck her. "All right," she said. "I'll pray with you—right here, right now—if you'll allow me to pray for you as well."

Rapture Pigott grinned, and his eyes crinkled with delight. "You bet, Sister!" he said triumphantly. "And you won't be sorry; you'll see. Jesus will meet you right here in this cafe, and your life will never be the same again."

He stopped suddenly as Sister Gertrude laid her left hand on his arm, crossed herself with her right, and began to pray aloud—in Latin.

From behind him, Mavis Kitchens' voice said quietly, "She's a nun, Pigott. The new nun at St. Sebaldus."

Rapture Pigott jumped up as if Mavis had just poured a pot of scalding coffee in his lap. He stared down at Sister Gertrude, who had paused in her prayer and was looking up at him with a benign expression of goodwill.

"Don't leave yet, Mr. Pigott," she said softly. "I'm quite experienced at doing battle with Protestant infidels."

&

Rapture ran for the door with the laughter of the multitudes ringing in his ears. He dashed outside, panting. For a moment he stood there dazed, wondering what on earth had happened. He brushed at his arm—the sleeve contaminated by the Papist nun's touch—and squinted into the sun. He had left his seed-corn cap behind, still perched on the napkin dispenser at the nun's table.

Then it came to him. Jesus, after all, had been despised and rejected of men. Did he expect any less, since he was a servant of the Most High?

His heart lifted as he thought of the Man of Sorrows, doing battle with the Enemy of Souls in the wilderness. He had been faithful, had done his part. The rest was up to God. She still had the tract, after all. And who could know what the Lord might do in her life because of Rapture Pigott's witness?

He smiled and shook the dust of the place from his feet.When Sunday came at First Freewill Holiness Church, he would still have something important to share. He could tell how he had risked everything to offer the gospel to a Catholic nun, only to be persecuted for righteousness' sake.

⁂

Citizen of the Year

For whoever exalts himself will be humbled, and whoever humbles himself will be exalted."
—Matthew 23:12

MACKENZIE HUBER picked up the *Angstrom County Chronicle,* lying in its accustomed place beside his bowl of bran flakes. His wife, Estelle, poured his coffee and pointed over his shoulder to the half-page article on the "Community Events" page.

HUBER NOMINATED AS CITIZEN OF THE YEAR, the banner headline read. A grainy picture showed Mac Huber, flanked by the mayor and the hospital director, standing under the dedication plaque for the children's wing of the new hospital in Marshall Forks. The three men smiled blandly at the camera, their arms draped over one another's shoulders.

Mac peered at the photograph, a slow smile spreading over his face. "Don't look too bad for an old man," he murmured, pleased with the contrast between his own trim image and the lumpish, balding figures of his two counterparts.

At fifty-nine, MacKenzie Huber was, physically speaking, a man to be reckoned with. He maintained the physique of a man twenty-five years his junior, jogging daily along the trails of Blue River Park and playing racquetball twice a week at the community health club where his name was engraved on a brass plaque reserved for "Centennial Contributors."

Mac's name was, in fact, engraved on almost every plaque in town. He gave generously to local charities, sponsored fund drives, and ran annually in the Tri-County Marathon. The media loved him; he cut an imposing figure on the ten o'clock news, his mane of silver hair streaming in the wind as he ran, his tanned, muscular legs outstripping the equipment-burdened reporters who struggled along beside him. Any comment from Mac Huber made the evening report, even on a subject as innocuous as the marathon. Everyone expected him to be running a different kind of race when the fall primaries rolled around.

"Sweetheart..." Estelle's voice, gently insistent, roused Mac from his thoughts. "It's getting late, and—"

"I know, I know," he responded automatically, curtly. "Where's my briefcase? I've got a meeting with Hartlet at ten."

"On the deacon's bench in the hall, as usual," Estelle replied, removing the half-eaten bowl of soggy bran flakes from the table. "Will you be home in time for dinner?"

"Doubt it," he muttered. "Don't wait."

Estelle sat down at the table beside him and laid a hand on his arm. "Mac," she began, "I think we need to talk. You've been so caught up in business lately, and I understand that, but—"

He moved his arm abruptly, shaking off the pressure of her hand. "Estelle, don't," he said. "You know I don't have time for this. If I intend to run for office next term—and we agreed that I should, remember—I have to lay the groundwork now. Make contacts, keep myself in the public eye. And," he finished, slapping a tanned hand down on the newspaper, "being named Citizen of the Year won't hurt any, either."

"Of course not, dear," Estelle replied in a quiet voice. "But Citizen of the Year is an honor; you don't have to *campaign* for it."

"Who are you kidding?" he snapped. "Just what do you think is going on out there in the real world? Whatever you get, you earn. Citizen of the Year, Mayor, Governor, Senator—it's all the same. And I—"

Suddenly he stopped, and both his countenance and his voice softened. "Estelle," he said wearily, "I care about this town, this state. I want to *do* something productive, to contribute something. I want to be known as a man who left behind an inheritance, a legacy of decent living and moral value. I can do that; I can give something back. And that's exactly what I intend to do."

Huber made for the door, grabbed his briefcase from the bench, and turned in the open doorway to face his wife. "Give me a little space, Estelle, please. This is important. When the campaign is over, things will be different; you'll see."

He gave her a quick kiss on the cheek and loped down the sidewalk toward his car, gone too quickly to hear her sigh, "No, Mac, it won't be different. It never has been."

ஐ

On the lower side of Turner's Crossroads, between a second-hand clothing store and an ancient vacuum cleaner repair shop, stood an open space of grass known informally as Sylvan Green. When the old Sylvan's Department Store had been demolished a year ago, the space had stood empty, like the dark gap of a missing tooth. For seven months the mounds of earth and demolition trash lured the local schoolboys with the seductive call of forbidden territory. There, among broken beer bottles and splintered boards full of rusty nails, the youth of the lower side played out their battle-games.

But the wounds of war were all too real—a three-inch nail through the sole of a bare foot; two broken arms; a kneecap cut to the bone. The City Fathers expressed their concern; every quarter, a motion lay on the table to "do something" about the vacant lot. Every quarter, the motion was tabled for lack of funds.

Then, as if by magic, something began to happen. Boards and bottles began to disappear from the Sylvan lot. Dirt mounds evened out into gently rolling hills. Grass seed, scattered at night, began to take root. Four or five seedling trees appeared, and among them, a winding gravel path. When the wrought-iron fence began to appear, a section at a time, the lower town residents could stand the mystery no longer. All night a delegation waited, huddled in the window of Marsell's Drug Store across the street. Nothing happened. At two a.m., tired and grouchy, they all went home to their beds.

The next morning, the fence was completed, stretching between the flanking buildings, with a narrow gate opening onto the path. Several small park benches stood in the curves of the path and the shelter of the hills.

No one in lower town knew how Sylvan Green had come about, or who was responsible. Eventually they stopped trying to figure it out and simply enjoyed the place, picnicking on the grass with their families, sitting on the hillside in the evening breeze, waiting for sunset. They kept it clean, took turns mowing and raking, and every spring set aside a Saturday to repaint the fence and the benches. For most of them, Sylvan Green became a symbol of hope, a sign that they were not forgotten.

❧

Estelle Huber had discovered Sylvan Green on her first trip to the second-hand store on Randolph Street. She had come on a charity mission for her husband, bringing four of Mac's old wide-lapel suits and a box of ancient flare-leg trousers, along with a trash bag full of her boys' clothes. Some they had outgrown; others were simply out of favor—last year's colors, or bearing the wrong logo. Still usable, but refused by her fashion-conscious brood, whole wardrobes were discarded into the "charity bin" and brought to lower town, where people really needed them.

"Get a tax receipt," Mac had instructed, handing her an itemized list. "We need all the deductions we can get. Besides, it helps to have a record of our donations."

But Estelle had forgotten the tax receipt. She entered Randolph Street Resurrections expecting to find a dim-lit, dreary store smelling of mothballs and old wool. Instead, she discovered a bright, well-ordered shop, charming in its mismatched decor. Castoff furniture was arranged in room settings—a living room here, complete with scatter rugs, lamps, and tables; a bedroom over in the corner, the scarred dresser covered with a hand-embroidered scarf, the bed adorned with an off-white chenille spread, obviously used, but of superior quality.

Most charming of all was Standard Brown, the owner and manager of Randolph Street Resurrections. A tall, graceful woman with skin the color of old oak, she greeted the visitor in the doorway in a low, gentle, musical voice. "Come in, Ma'am," she said. "I am Standard Brown, the owner of this establishment."

"Uh...Standard?" Estelle stammered, caught off guard both by the atmosphere of the store and the refinement of its proprietor.

Standard threw back her head and laughed—not loud, but deep and ringing, like church chimes. "Yes, Lord," she chuckled. "When I was just a child, folks in the fellowship said I used to sing a song about lifting up the standard on the mountain. It sorta stuck, and they been calling me Standard ever since."   She shook her head pensively and added, as if talking to herself, "Don't guess I knew then what it meant. But I know now, Lord, I know now."

Standard advanced to where Estelle still stood in the doorway and put a gentle hand across her shoulders. "Come on in, dear." Estelle inhaled deeply, and a scent of clean soap and lavender filled her senses.

"I—I brought some things for you," she whispered. Somehow, in this environment, with this woman, Estelle felt a little ashamed of her offering of charity. She wished she could bolt for the door and leave, but her sweaty fist still clamped around the trash bag full of cast-off clothes.

Suddenly Standard was all business. She strode over to an old desk and sat down, pulling out a legal pad, pen, and calculator. "Well, then, let's see what we've got." She smiled up at Estelle, holding the pen in her long fingers.

"I have a list," Estelle murmured, producing Mac's itemization, wrinkled and damp, from the hand still gripping the trash bag.

"That's very thoughtful of you," Standard murmured. "It will save both of us a lot of time. Perhaps you'd like to look around a bit while I sort through these things."

"Yes...thank you," Estelle managed. She walked quickly away, turning her eyes from the familiar jeans and sweaters Standard was removing from the bag. This was all wrong—wrong, somehow, for her to be here, offering a condescending charity to this woman who received it with so much grace and elegance.

Estelle wandered over to the bedroom setting and began fingering the embroidered dresser cloth. It was beautiful work, pastel flowers and birds, with a hand-crocheted edging—very much like the piecework she remembered seeing at her grandmother's house when she was very young.

"It's lovely, isn't it?" A lyrical voice at her elbow interrupted Estelle's thoughts.

"Yes, it is. Like the things my grandmother used to make. It reminds me...of a simpler life, somehow."

"Life these days is rarely simple," Standard mused. "Guess we take simple pleasures wherever we can find them."

Estelle had no answer. She turned and looked into Standard's eyes, brown and alive, like a flowing river after a rainstorm. "And do you find such pleasures here?" she asked, with a candor and vulnerability that astonished both of them.

"Yes," said Standard simply. "This is a very good place to be."

The woman's dark eyes held Estelle's blue ones for a moment until Estelle could stand the intensity of the gaze no longer. She looked away, and the momentary bond was broken.

"These clothes are quite nice," Standard said suddenly. "Somebody will get a lot of good out of them."

Estelle didn't want to talk about the clothes, but Standard pressed on. "I can give you a receipt for the value," she said. "If you want cash, forty dollars for the lot."

"Cash?" Estelle jerked her head up, forcing herself to focus on the smooth brown skin instead of the intense dark eyes. "No, no, I—"

"A receipt then," the woman replied. "In what name?"

Estelle paused. For a moment she panicked, wishing desperately that she could avoid giving the name. "MacKenzie Huber," she admitted finally.

"Ah," Standard breathed.

A moment of silence lay between them, a persistent oppression. Finally Standard Brown spoke.

"Mrs. Huber—"

"Estelle. Please call me Estelle." She caught the brown eyes again, and they were once more alive with understanding.

"Estelle. Would you have lunch with me?"

Estelle breathed a sigh of relief and nodded eagerly. "I'd love to."

❧

Lunch consisted of turkey sandwiches on thick brown bread. The two women sat together on a bench in Sylvan Green. Estelle fed crusts to a squirrel who ventured down out of his tree while Standard explained to her the genesis of the park, and how it had become the center of community for the lower town residents.

Across the green from Randolph Street Resurrections, high on the side of the vacuum cleaner repair shop, a young man stood on a makeshift scaffolding, a long board propped between two ladders. With great care, he was painting a mural on the side of the building—a pastoral scene of woods and streams that blended perfectly into the actual landscaping of Sylvan

Green and seemed to extend its beauty on forever.

"Who pays that man to paint?" Estelle asked.

"Lord, Lord, no one *pays* him!" Standard laughed. "That's my son, Regis. He works at the loading docks and goes to school at night; but Thursday's his day off, and he spends it here, painting. When he's done over there, he'll start on my side."

She pointed behind them at the side of her shop, an ugly, windowless brick wall.

"All the stores on this street were connected," she explained. "When they tore down Sylvan's Department Store, these side walls were left like an open wound. Regis is helping to heal them." Standard smiled into Estelle's eyes, unself-conscious of the poetic image in her words.

"That's beautiful," Estelle said.

"Yes, it is," Standard replied, gazing at her son's handiwork. He is a talented young man, and I am very proud of him."

"No," Estelle protested, "I meant—" She stopped suddenly. "Standard," she said, "why didn't you ask the City for help in renovation down here?"

A dark shadow moved across the brown face. "The subject came up, I reckon. But it seems that the people on the City Council were more concerned about projects for health clubs in uptown—"

"People like my husband, you mean," Estelle interjected wearily.

Standard reached over and took Estelle's pale hand in her dark, smooth fingers. "No matter," she said gently. "It worked out best in the end. If the City don't help, then we help ourselves. Brings folks together."

Estelle clutched Standard's hand in a vise-like hold, just as the idea gripped her mind in a blinding flash of revelation.

"Standard," she gasped, riveting the brown eyes with her own. "It was you, wasn't it? You did—"

"Shush," Standard rebuked her. "Don't ask such a thing." Tears filled her eyes, and one slid down her cheek, making a shiny brown track on the side of her nose. She smiled, and the effect was like sunshine in the midst of a spring rain. "This is a place of beauty," she whispered, "a place of simple pleasures. Don't need to know anything else."

⁂

MacKenzie Huber struggled with his tie, then jerked it off in frustration. "Estelle!" he roared. "Will you come help me with this thing—please!"

Estelle came out of the bathroom in time to see her husband pacing up and down the length of the bedroom, his tie yanked into an impossible knot. "Whoever invented this penguin suit ought to be shot," he protested.

"Now, dear," she soothed. "You look very handsome in a tuxedo. And the tie is a simple matter." She pushed him to a sitting position on the bed, then sat down and began working on the bow tie from behind, her arms around his neck.

"Listen to this," he commanded, pulling a folded sheet of paper out of his vest pocket. "Friends and colleagues, it is with great pleasure and thankfulness that I accept the honor of being named Citizen of the Year. I am humbled and awed by your faith in me, and I vow to return that faith by serving this community with even greater zeal and enthusiasm." He paused, twisting around to try to see her face. "Well, how does that sound?"

Estelle closed her eyes tightly for a moment and exhaled a long breath. "That's very nice, dear," she replied. "There, your tie is done." She patted his back briefly, sighed, and went back into the bathroom.

❧

The Citizen of the Year banquet, held in the main ballroom of the Blue River Country Club, drew all the prominent citizens from three surrounding counties— every mayor of every small town, every politician campaigning for election, all the rich and famous and aspiring to be so. And all of them—from the busboys to the news anchors—expected to see MacKenzie Huber receive the coveted award.

Estelle and Mac sat at the table closest to the speaker's platform—front and center, just inside the illuminated circle cast by the spotlight. Mac, the center of attention at the table, talked incessantly with those around him. Estelle sat quietly through four courses, waiting.

At last the house lights dimmed and the chairman of the Citizens' Committee, Harry Franklin, stood squinting into the spotlight. Conversation died to a low buzz, then ceased altogether as Harry began to speak.

He went on forever, it seemed, droning about the importance of community service to Turner's Crossroads, while Mac smiled and elbowed those on either side of him. At last Franklin got to the point.

"We're here tonight, as you know, to honor someone who has been of great service to the community." He waited for the expected applause, and when he was satisfied with the response, continued. "This year's recipient of the Citizen of the Year award is a person who has unselfishly given time and great effort to make this community a better place to live. We learned of this individual's activities through an anonymous but eloquent letter delivered to the committee a few weeks ago...."

Mac wasn't listening; he had fished his notes for his acceptance speech out of his vest pocket and was silently mouthing the words.

"And with no thought of any recognition, tonight's honoree worked tirelessly at a thankless and financially unrewarding task—making a garden of simple pleasures in a most unlikely place."

Estelle smiled. Franklin was quoting verbatim from the letter.

"And so tonight we honor an unsung heroine among us—"

Heroine? The crowd began to murmur, and Franklin elevated his voice to be heard above the noise.

"This year's Citizen of the Year award goes to—"

Mac stood up, the spotlight flooding his tanned face and silver mane of hair. He was smiling, and put his hand up to wave to the crowd.

"Mrs. Standard Brown!"

The crowd began to titter, then full-scale laughing broke out. Mac looked around, and at last the full impact of what was happening hit him. He paled under his tan, then his neck began to redden, flushing upward to his ears. Abruptly he sat down again, dropping his acceptance speech into his water glass.

The spotlight swung around to the back of the room. There, threading her way among the tables, came a regal-looking woman in a long dress, her skin the color of old oak, her dark eyes glistening with unshed tears. Escorting her was a young man with the same eyes, the same skin, the same gentle demeanor. He was wearing, not a tuxedo, but a dark suit with wide lapels and flare-leg pants.

As the woman approached the platform, she paused a moment, front and center, and held Estelle's blue eyes with her dark gaze.

"It was you, wasn't it?" she whispered.

"Shush, Standard," Estelle replied. "Don't ask such a thing."

The smooth brown fingers clutched Estelle's pale hand. Standard leaned down and kissed Estelle's cheek, pressing a small packet into her palms.

Estelle never heard Standard's words of acceptance. The low, deep, gentle voice rang softly in the background, like church chimes, as Estelle tore open the package. There, wrapped in delicate tissue-paper, lay the dresser-scarf, its pastel design bordered with a hand-crocheted edging. Inside the first fold was a delicately-written note: *For the simple pleasures. Lift up the Standard.*

Estelle sensed movement around her and looked up. Everyone, except for MacKenzie Huber, had risen to applaud the Citizen of the Year.

❧

A Sure and
Certain Witness

As it is written, "God's name is blasphemed among the Gentiles because of you...."
—Romans 2:24

WHEN ELIZABETH and Marcus Reardon took over Gram Reardon's farm, behind Manny Fisher's place on the outskirts of Turner's Crossroads, they expected to enter into a life of peace and serenity. They were the logical Reardons for Gram to leave the place to; she had held onto the land for fourteen years after Pap's demise, and she willed it to them jointly.

"You kids," she told Marcus and Liz the week before she died, "are the only grandchildren I've got who have sense enough to take care of this place.

Everybody else in this blamed family's gone up to Minneapolis or out to Arizona to build jailhouses in the desert. Ha!"

Gram was referring, of course, to Tracy, Aunt Libba's oldest boy, who was making a fortune contracting expensive condos in an exclusive retirement community in Scottsdale. But she could never understand why anybody would deliberately choose to live where trees couldn't grow, so she went to her grave swearing that her grandson built prison cells—tortuous hotboxes for incorrigible criminals.

Gram was right about one thing, though—nobody else in the family gave two hoots about "the place," as everybody called it. It was a wonderful old homestead, thirty acres on the north fork of the Blue River.

Reardon Farm would have been attractive to the other relatives, of course, if it could have been sold for cash. But the property had only a dozen acres or so of tillable land; most of it was river bottom and swamp and what old Pap Reardon called "squirrel woods," good for nothing except peace and solitude and long walks in the autumn. Besides, it was covenanted for homesteading, written into all the wills. Pap and his daddy before him had made sure of that. So there was nothing left to do when Gram died but to let Marcus and Liz take it over.

The farm—and the community of Turner's Crossroads—couldn't have been more perfect for Marcus and Liz. From the days when Gram and Pap lived there with his parents, there were two houses on the place, adequately spaced out on ten acres of woodland. Twelve acres were rented out to farm soybeans, and the remaining eight acres or so was river backwater—a swamp forming a natural barrier against the backside of Manny Fisher's acreage.

Marcus wasn't interested in farming, but he loved the old place—loved its history and its heritage and its tranquility. He had come back from Viet Nam in 1973 with a permanent limp and a pervasive melancholy. It had taken him ten years to "find himself," to cut his hair and trim his beard and sell his Harley and settle down. But finally, seven years into a marriage that began in rough waters, he and Liz were adjusting to parenthood and ready to make a life for themselves—and for their daughter, Markie, age four.

"This will be perfect for us," Marcus had said the day Gram Reardon's will was read. "Little Markie can grow up in the country; I can set up shop, and you can help with the refinishing and sell crafts."

"Setting up shop" for Marcus meant moving his antique business and finding a suitable location to sell and refinish furniture. Business had been bad for him in the past few years. He had determined to move, and inheriting the farm had given him the chance he'd been waiting for. He and Liz had both grown up in Angstrom County; taking over Reardon Farm was like coming home.

It was the chance Liz had prayed for, too—but she had never told her husband the direction of her prayers. Marcus was a fine man, a moral man with high standards of integrity and a deep commitment to his family. But he had never quite gotten over his bitterness and depression about his experiences in the war. Liz hoped—in fact, she stormed the gates of heaven daily—that somehow, in some way, Marcus would realize his need for a personal faith.

A long time ago, Liz had stopped talking to Marcus about faith. "We both grew up in the same church," he'd say, "so I guess I've heard about all there is to hear. And it seems to me that those who talk the loudest about their Christianity end up being the ones who show it least. It's what goes on between Monday and Saturday that really counts."

She couldn't argue with him—after all, he was right. And he had had plenty of bad experiences with people who called themselves Christians. Even the news reports seemed to confirm Marcus's conclusions about the church. But she was hoping that now, with things looking up for them, he'd come to see the light and change his mind about religion.

Gram Reardon's big house needed a lot of work to make it livable—wallpaper, painting, fixing bathrooms, refinishing the oak woodwork. Liz had promised Marcus the perfectionist that they would "do it right" instead of "remuddling." It would likely take a year or more to finish.

So initially, while the work was being done on the big Victorian farmhouse, they moved into the "Old House." The Old House began as a cabin built of logs, hand-hewed by Great-grandpa Reardon and erected as one room with a lean-to kitchen in 1863. The log house had been built onto time after time, and the end result over a hundred years later was a patchwork of a place, with ground floor rooms at four different levels and a second floor that could only be reached by an outside stairway.

Marcus thought it was perfect; it was sound and sturdy, and likely to last another hundred years. In the first three months, he had already rewired, replaced the plumbing, and taken the log room back to the natural wood.

"Soon as I get this house livable," he said one night, staring into the flames of the fire he had built in the open stone fireplace, "I'm gonna set up a real nice shop, get my stuff out of storage, and start making some contacts with other antique dealers. You know, I've been looking around, and a lot of the furniture and tools I have might be in real demand here.

"I've thought, too, Liz," he went on as he stirred the fire with an iron poker, "that maybe I might get the chance to do some artistic stuff—some woodcarving, making special furniture pieces, that kind of thing."

"It'll be good for both of us, won't it, Marcus, just to find a place to call home—a place to be what we're meant to be?" Liz looked up at his handsome bearded face, and her heart wrenched with a bittersweet joy. They had come so far; maybe now, after all the struggle, things would finally go right for them. Perhaps they would come home spiritually as well.

&

At six one Sunday morning, Liz was making coffee when she heard the sound of a sledge hammer driving a wedge into wood. She went out the back door in her bathrobe, coffee cup in hand, to find Marcus splitting logs for the fireplace.

"You want some coffee?" she shouted above the rhythmic thump of the hammer.

"Sure." He set the hammer against the log pile and retrieved his flannel shirt from the limb of a tree. When Liz came back with a second cup of steaming coffee, he was sitting on the steps waiting. She handed him a cup and settled down beside him on the step.

"Is Markie up yet?" His breath from the hot coffee smoked against the cool morning air.

Liz shook her head. "I thought I'd let her sleep."

Marcus smiled and put an arm around her, drawing her close and giving her a coffee-flavored kiss. "Well, then, we'll just enjoy the morning together," he said. "When she gets up, how about if we take a walk down to the old barn by the river? I've been thinking that, since it's visible from the road, I might be able to fix it up and use that for my shop...." His words dwindled into silence as he caught the expression in her eyes.

"What's wrong?" he said at last.

"Nothing, Marcus, it's just—" She faltered. "Well, I mean, it's Sunday, and, I thought I'd—"

"Go to church?" His voice carried just an edge of hardness.

"Marcus, you know church fellowship is important to me. I just thought maybe that—"

"That I might go with you this time." He looked down at his scuffed work boots and kicked at a splinter working its way out of the step.

She hesitated. When he raised his head, his brown eyes were soft, filled with tender emotion. "Liz," he said quietly, "I know I haven't always been the ideal husband—"

She tried to protest, but he stopped her with a wave of his hand. "Let me finish. I haven't been the easiest man to live with, and you've loved me through the worst of it. But you know I've struggled with church. I didn't see much evidence of God in Nam. Oh, I saw men slogging up to their waists in the swamp, terrified of being blown to bits or having their brains fried with Agent Orange. I heard a lot of foxhole prayers. But when the shooting stopped, most of them went back to being just like they were before."

He paused and ran a hand through his hair. When he spoke again, his voice was a whisper, filled with the unspeakable weariness of a man who has seen too much. "I never saw anything in church that would make me believe in a God who had any power to deal with reality. It all seemed like a farce, a game played by people who didn't want to face up to the darkness in their own souls."

Liz drew her robe closer around her and leaned against him, waiting. They had had this conversation before. He had never stood in the way of her faith, but he had never sought it for himself.

Marcus turned to her, smiling. "I don't know what it is, Liz—maybe it's this place, the peace and security of it." He sighed, looking out across the clearing to the woods beyond. "But somehow I'm beginning to feel that maybe there is a God who can bring peace into all the turmoil." He laughed lightly as her jaw dropped in astonishment. "Surprised?" he said. "Well, maybe there's hope even for someone like me." He squeezed her hand, and his gaze wandered once again to the awakening woods. "There's a peace in this place," he said at last. "A healing kind of peace. If it's God's doing, I guess I should at least give Him a chance...."

༄

Liz left Markie with her father and drove into Turner's Crossroads to church, hoping to find a small pocket of spiritual life in this country town. Gram Reardon had attended the First Presbyterian Church, but Liz had heard from her that Crossroads Baptist had had some sort of revival in the past two or three years, and everybody around town was talking about the changes.

She pulled into the parking lot, feeling that strange sensation that one only gets in a small town—the feeling of being isolated and yet, at the same time, the center of attention. Everybody knew Liz was new in town, and everybody, it seemed, already knew her name, occupation, place of residence, and reason for moving to Turner's Crossroads.

"Reardon, is it?" one ancient man shouted, pumping Liz's hand. "Bess Reardon's grandson's living out on the old place—you any relation?" Liz opened her mouth to answer, but he continued to pump, his spotted fist gripping hers. "Old Bess was a real looker in her day, I can tell you!" He squealed with delight, and shuffled off to find a seat.

The worship service was simple, enthusiastic, and filled with music. The sermon, fifty-two minutes' worth, was strictly expository preaching with a minimum of emotionalism, punctuated by a few appropriately placed "Amens." By the time the choir of ten sang the final benediction, Liz was ready to come back for the evening prayer meeting.

As the congregation began to file out, rustling jackets and bulletins, a smiling couple turned to her from the pew directly in front. "Welcome to Crossroads Baptist," the man said. He was of medium height with brown hair thinning at the temples and a broad, upswept mustache. "I'm R.C. Christiansen, and this is my wife, Patti."

"Patti with an *i*," the blonde woman at his side said.

"Don't I know you? I'm Elizabeth Reardon."

"Liz Reardon, yes—you married old Mrs. Reardon's grandson!" The man beamed. "I heard you and your husband had inherited the old place." He looked around expectantly.

"Marcus isn't here today," she explained lamely.

"Well, well—Liz Reardon! I'm Bobby Chuck. Don't you remember? We used to play ball together!"

Suddenly it all came back to her—Robert Charles Christiansen, Angstrom County's fair-haired boy. Liz hadn't seen him in over twenty-five years, but if she had thought of him, she would have expected him to be somewhere else besides the Baptist church in Turner's Crossroads. Bobby Chuck, as she recalled, had never set foot inside a church as a teenager; he had insisted quite vocally that he would "shake off the dust of this one-horse town and never be caught dead in Turner's Crossroads again." Yet here he was, to all appearances, very much alive and quite entrenched in small-town life.

"Well, I hardly expected to see you again, after almost thirty years! Marcus and I have been here fairly often, taking care of Gram after Papaw died. Why haven't we run into you?"

"Well, just different circles, I guess. Your grandmother, of course, went to the Presbyterian church. And I—well, it's only been in the past few years that I've been here myself. Say! Why don't you come to dinner, and we can catch up." His wife threw him a sidelong glance, and then nodded.

"Yes, do come," she said.

⁂

Liz called home and got no answer—apparently Marcus was down at the barn with Markie. She left a message on the answering machine, and with some misgivings accompanied the Christiansens to their sprawling, elaborate ranch-style home on a hill overlooking town.

Dinner with the Christiansens proved a profitable use of the early part of Sunday afternoon. R.C., as he now chose to be called, gave her a detailed account of his conversion and subsequent marriage to Patti with an *i*, his second wife. After the failure of his first marriage and ten years of dog-eat-dog business down in Des Moines, he had abandoned the fast lane to return home to Turner's Crossroads. Here he had met the Lord and Patti all in one fell swoop, and he had established himself as a local contractor and builder. He advertised his business as KingsWay Building, Inc.

"And I perceive," he concluded, focusing intently upon Liz, "that you, too, have had a life-changing confrontation with the Lord."

"Well, yes," she answered, uncomfortable under his

gaze, "I became a Christian in college."

"And then you married Marcus?"

"We kept in touch during the seventies," she answered evasively. "A couple of years after he got home from Viet Nam, we finally got married. He, uh...had some things to work through."

R.C.'s brow knitted with concern. "Yes, yes, we had heard he had some...trouble...from his time in Southeast Asia."

Word gets around, Liz thought. *I guess small towns never change.*

When Liz returned home, she told Marcus about her dinner and conversation with the Christiansens.

"Yeah, I know 'em," he said cryptically. "Boober Chuck and his little wife, Putti. He barely gives me the time of day on the street—acts like he doesn't remember me at all." He paused, and his tone softened. "But maybe, now that they've met up with you again, things will be different."

&

On Saturday morning two weeks later, as Marcus was loading tools and lumber into his truck to take down to the barn, he looked up to see a caravan of cars and trucks pulling up in the driveway. Twenty-three men and eleven of their wives appeared, the men in jeans with tool belts slung on their hips, the wives carrying covered-dish casseroles.

"We came to help," R.C. Christiansen announced, stepping forward from the crowd. "With all of us working, we'll get your barn ready for you to set up shop in no time."

By dusk Saturday evening, the barn had a new floor, reinforced lofts, new stairs, and glass windows. One man had arrived with a road grader and another with a gravel truck, and before noon Marcus had a new gravel road from the barn door out to the main road, as well as a graveled parking lot in front of the door. The setting sun shone a golden light on the newly painted barn and, as a finishing touch, two men on parallel ladders hung an enormous sign against the broad barn wall: REARDON'S FURNITURE AND ANTIQUES.

Marcus was impressed. "Liz," he said when everybody was gone and he finally had a chance to sit down with her, "I've never seen anything like it. Where did all those people come from?"

"Crossroads Baptist," she replied. "R.C. Christiansen rounded them up."

"Boober Chuck?" Marcus always distorted R. C.'s childhood nickname, and R.C. was always irritated by the affront to his dignity. "Well, maybe the man has changed. Maybe I should give him the benefit of the doubt."

"Maybe so," Liz said. "They've invited both of us to dinner tomorrow night."

※

To Liz's surprise, Marcus agreed to go. He put on clean khakis, a navy polo shirt, and loafers. And as they got in the truck to leave, he turned to her and said, "Sweetheart, I'm going for you, but I hope it turns out to be for me, too."

During dinner, R.C. and Marcus began discussing

Marcus's plans for his business. "I want to thank you for all your help on the barn," Marcus said, his voice full of genuine warmth. "It will be perfect for my antique and refinishing business." He paused and looked down at the table, toying with his food. "I just...don't know why you would do such a thing for me."

"Didn't do it for you," R.C. boomed. He winked at Liz. "Did it for Jesus."

Marcus shifted in his chair and said nothing.

"One of the wonderful things about being a Christian," R.C. went on, "is the call to help those who are less fortunate." Liz blanched, but R.C. didn't quit. "You know, when you have a personal relationship with Jesus, it just makes you want to love everybody, and to do good for others. You know."

"Yeah," Marcus said.

"Now, I'll tell you what," R.C. continued. "You're gonna need some advertising—signs up on the main highway, that kind of thing."

Marcus shrugged. "I guess so. I haven't really had a chance to—"

"You've seen my billboards up on the interstate, advertising KingsWay Builders?" R.C. interrupted.

Marcus nodded.

"I've got a couple of guys who are real experts—they do all my advertising signs. I'll call them tomorrow and make arrangements for them to do up a couple of big signs for you."

"Well, that's really nice of you, R.C., but—"

"No objections, now. You're worried about the cost, am I right? Well, don't give it a second thought.

I'll run it through my business account, write it off as business expense...you'll only have to pay for the materials. Couple hundred bucks, tops."

"Is that legal?" Marcus said, raising an eyebrow at Liz across the table.

R.C. slanted a conspiratorial glance at his wife. "Well, now, we'll just make it legal, won't we? We'll get you all fixed up, old man—you'll see."

≈

Later that night, sitting in front of the fire in the log house, Marcus tried to sort out what had happened during the dinner at R.C Christiansen's.

"He's being really nice and...helpful," Marcus said. "But he's so...I don't know...pushy."

Liz linked her arm through his and squeezed. "It's just his way, Sweetheart," she said. "He's just trying to help." An unnamed doubt nagged at her, but she shoved it aside. R.C. was, after all, showing an abundance of Christian love to Marcus—no doubt more than he had ever seen. The man *was* pushy, that was the truth. And she questioned some of his methods. But in the process, he was giving Marcus a clear testimony of faith in action. What more could she want?

≈

Marcus went to church with Liz the following Sunday; throughout the month of September he tried, as he said, to give R.C. and the others at Crossroads Baptist the benefit of the doubt.

On the last Monday in September, he prepared to leave for Marshall Forks to meet with the advertising manager of the *Angstrom County Chronicle* to set up ads for the grand opening of Reardon Furniture and Antiques, scheduled for October 15. "It'll be the peak of the color season," Marcus explained to Liz. "People will be driving down all weekend to see the fall colors. It's a perfect time for the grand opening."

He showed her a mock-up of the advertisement—a quarter-page spread with some nice graphics of antiques and furniture around the border. *GRAND OPENING—REARDON FURNITURE AND ANTIQUES,* the copy read. *FOLLOW THE SIGNS FROM THE HIGHWAY TO THE BIG RED BARN.*

"It's perfect!" Liz said. "With the signs up on the highway, they can't miss it."

"About the signs," Marcus said. "Has R.C. told you when they'll be put up?"

"No, but while you're gone I'll go down and check with him. He knows the grand opening is in two weeks. I'm sure he's got everything under control."

Marcus stood up and gathered the ad copy into a manila folder. "I gotta go," he said. "I'll be back by dark." He took Liz into his arms and kissed her, then leaned back to look into her face. "You know, Sweetheart, I've got a feeling this is the beginning of a whole new life for us." He sighed and smiled, a faraway look filling his eyes. "And I have to admit, R.C. has been a big help to us. I can't believe all those guys who worked on the barn came back last Tuesday to help unload the truck when the antiques arrived."

Liz nodded and smiled. Her heart soared; she had never seen Marcus so excited, so...positive. For two weeks she had seen no sign of that dark melancholic side of his personality. *Let it last, Dear Lord*, she prayed silently. *Let this be a new beginning—for both of us.*

After Marcus left, Liz took Markie and drove into town. They played for a while in the park, then walked up the hill to the Christiansen house. It was a beautiful brisk fall day; the leaves on the trees were just beginning to turn. Marcus was right: two weeks would bring them to peak color, the perfect time for his grand opening.

When Liz knocked on the door, Patti opened immediately.

"Come in!" boomed R. C.'s unmistakable voice from the dining room. "Sit down—have some coffee and a piece of Patti's wonderful coffee cake."

"I came to check on the signs," Liz ventured after two cups of coffee. "Marcus has gone up to Marshall Forks to arrange for the newspaper ads, and he wanted to make sure the signs would be up on the highway in time for the grand opening."

Patti paled visibly, but said nothing. Finally R.C. cleared his throat and said, "Well, yes, the signs. You know, Liz, I've been busy with *paying* propositions—"

"Like jobs he's contracting for," interjected Patti.

"And, well, I just haven't gotten around to finishing up the arrangements about the signs yet."

"R.C.!" Liz gasped, trying to restrain herself. "You promised that the signs would be up already, and now you're telling me they're not even painted! Marcus is planning on a big grand opening—"

R.C. laughed indulgently and clasped his hands behind his head. "Of course, Liz. But you understand how these things are. Everything takes time. Aren't you willing to trust the Lord for the timing of this?"

"Trust the Lord!" Liz spluttered. "The Lord's no problem—but you—you promised my husband you'd have the signs done, and now—"

"It's only a couple of signs, Liz. Don't panic; we'll get it done. Why, if you knew the things the Lord has called me to do lately...and besides, we still have two weeks. Trust me; the signs will be up, and they will be beautiful. People will be flocking in here to the grand opening of Reardon's Antiques!"

❧

October 15 dawned, a bright and beautiful autumn Saturday, with a chill in the air and the glory of fall colors in the canopy of leaves overhead. The cool dampness made Marcus's injured leg ache, but nothing could mar the joy of the morning. He breathed in the musky scent of the woods as he walked, kicking up leaves and laughing out loud at the slivers of deep blue sky against the gold and red of the maple trees.

Today marked more than the first day of his business; it was the culmination of a dream, the grand opening of his heart. Today, Marcus Reardon could almost believe that God heard his laughter, and smiled.

❧

With a heavy heart Marcus dragged his aching leg back through the woods and limped toward the house. Liz had a fire going; he could smell the woodsmoke mingled with the scent of steaks on the grill—their victory celebration.

All day long Marcus had heard the traffic up on the main highway, the whine of automobile tires against the pavement drifting down through the woods on the sweet autumn air. In ten hours, two cars had rounded the gravel driveway. One old couple had asked directions; a father with three small children had requested the use of the bathroom for his desperate six-year-old daughter. The cash box had remained closed; Marcus had not registered a single sale.

After a silent dinner, Marcus and Liz, with a sleepy Markie in the back seat, drove up to the highway and made a loop down the interstate and back. They passed four billboards advertising KingsWay Builders, Inc. Not a single sign in either direction pointed the way to Reardon's Furniture and Antiques.

🙚

At three-fifteen on Sunday afternoon. R.C. Christiansen and his wife, Patti (with an i), arrived at the Reardons' back door. Marcus opened the screen and stood in the doorway, blocking the entrance. There stood Boober Chuck and Putti, coffee cake in hand.

"Hey, Marcus," R.C. said. "We missed you in church this morning. I...uh, I wanted to let you know...uh, about the signs—well, my guys said they should be ready by the end of the week. They'll be up by next Saturday."

Marcus said nothing. He stood, holding onto the screen door, his eyes boring a hole into Boober Chuck's forehead.

"But, well, what's a week or so, right?" R.C. said. "I

mean, God's still in control, and His timing is perfect."

Marcus's jaw flinched. "I've been told that He usually keeps His promises," he said evenly.

"He sure does, old man!" R. C. returned jovially. "And it's a good thing. Because His servants, like me, well, we're not perfect, but we're forgiven!"

"Are you saying you were wrong?" pressed Marcus. "Wrong not to keep your word about the signs?"

"Well, c'mon Marcus," R. C. stammered, "I just kind of got behind—after all, we didn't have a written contract."

"I didn't think we needed one," Marcus replied.

"Well," faltered R.C. "I suppose we better get going, Patti. You'll get your signs, Reardon, old man," he said. "This week—absolutely. I'll see to it myself. You have my word."

"Oh, but Sweetie," Patti interrupted, "we've got dinner plans four nights this week—"

"Never mind that, Dear," he snarled. "Get back to me later in the week, Reardon, and we'll see how things are going."

R.C. led his wife by the arm down the steps and into the yard. Halfway to the sidewalk, he turned to Marcus and Liz, standing on the first two steps of the porch.

"By the way," R.C. called, "this Sunday is Fellowship Sunday. Since you're not members—yet—we'd like to invite both of you to be our guests at services and for dinner after church."

Marcus looked at Liz, his eyes shadowed with barely suppressed rage. "I don't think so, R.C.," he said. Then, under his breath, he muttered, "In fact, I'd say there's a snowball's chance in...."

R.C. turned and waved. "Maybe next time, then," he called. "Oh, by the way," he added as he opened the car door for Patti, "I'll have my guys send you a bill as soon as the signs are up. I got the work done for you pretty cheap—it came to, oh, I think just under nine hundred. You'll make it up in no time once your grand opening is underway."

Marcus didn't answer. He turned on his heel and went into the house, slamming the door behind him. Liz was still standing on the porch when R.C. came back across the yard.

"Maybe you better talk to him," R.C. said. "From what I just saw, your husband needs to learn a little about forgiveness." He looked up, a perplexed frown on his face. "I thought you said Marcus was open to the gospel, Liz."

"He was," Liz said, tears filling her eyes.

"Well, see if you can't get him there on Sunday," R.C. said. "I'm going to give my testimony, and I think he'd do well to hear it."

He started toward the car, where Patti sat waiting, still holding her offering of coffee cake. "We'll pray for him," he called back as he slid behind the wheel. "That man needs Jesus in his heart."

❧

Morning of the Broken Cross

There is a time for everything...a time to be silent, and a time to speak....
—Ecclesiastes 3:1,7

JANELLE SALEM unlatched the mullioned window and looked down to the cornfield below. Far away, so far that she couldn't hear the rustling of t he leaves or the raucous cry of the gulls as they hovered on the stiff breeze, she watched, as in a silent movie, the golden waves as they moved beneath the wind. She could feel the freshness of the early morning air, smell the dampness of the Blue River as it crested over the rapids known as Convent Falls, but the distance between herself and the river muffled the sound, and all she heard was a dull, steady roar, like static on an old tube radio.

The significance did not escape Janelle, and she sighed. For months now, perhaps for years, her hearing had been diminishing steadily. Her physical ears were unaffected; she still heard, all too plainly, the insistent ringing of the telephone, the noises of her children arguing, the plaintive cry of the puppy being dragged by his ears, the subdued muttering of her husband as he gave back one-word answers to her futile attempts at conversation.

But another Voice, the most important one in Janelle Salem's twenty-nine years, had fallen silent. Once upon a time, she had heard with remarkable clarity the whisper of her Beloved, sensed with unerring accuracy the direction of God's will. Even more, she *felt* that invisible presence with her, knew the Lord's love as a palpable embrace, the weight of God's longing for her fellowship.

Over the years the Voice had grown fainter, the presence more distant, like the river below her. She affirmed the truth of God's love, even as she accepted the reality of the waterfall; it was an objective absolute, fixed in her mind and heart. She believed, but she couldn't find that place of closeness anymore.

Janelle had mustered the courage to try to explain her dilemma to a few close people in her life. "Ron," she said to her husband, "I don't understand what's happening to me. I know all the right answers, do the right things, but God's presence seems to be slipping away."

"I wouldn't worry about it too much," Ron said. "I think it's an inevitable part of life, like losing that first romantic infatuation after you've been married a while."

Her sister Cecile said, "Janelle, you're being entirely too introspective. Why do you always have to probe around inside yourself like a surgeon looking for a new disease? You're a Christian, and you've got a good life and a happy family. I'd think you'd be satisfied with that."

Roxanne, Janelle's Bible study leader, had at least taken the matter seriously. "God isn't silent," she said. "We just sometimes refuse to hear Him. Let's pray and ask the Spirit to reveal whatever sin in your life is hindering you in your relationship with God. If you feel cut off from God, you can be sure you're the one who's moved away, not Him."

Janelle tried all the options: acceptance, positive thinking, confession. When nothing seemed to work, she went at last to her pastor. "God seems so far away," she told him, tears rising against her will. "What can I do to feel close again?"

Tenting his fingers and rocking back in his chair, the pastor thought for a moment. "You sound really depressed about this," he said. Janelle nodded. "The only cure I know for depression is to get involved helping other people. Service, that's the key. Serving Christ by serving others." He had signed her up to coordinate the Children's Church and to organize a Dorcas Guild to minister to the shut-ins. She entered dutifully into the work and never spoke another word to anyone about the pain in her heart.

At last, on the verge of complete burnout, Janelle had taken a final desperate step. She had heard of St. Sebaldus Convent, south of Turner's Crossroads overlooking the Blue River. There the nuns offered sanctuary to those desiring spiritual retreat. They provided room and board and solitude to anyone seeking a spiritual renewal.

Leaving Ron and the boys to fend for themselves, Janelle had driven from Marshall Forks down to St. Sebaldus five days ago. It was a last-ditch effort of sorts—a second honeymoon, intended to initiate a hoped-for restoration in a failing relationship. So far, the Bridegroom hadn't shown up.

Janelle was a Protestant, born and bred. Raised in a denomination that regarded the rituals of Catholicism as suspect, she found herself now battling against the old childhood prejudices. Everything seemed so strange, so foreign. Her days at the convent were bounded, morning and evening, by the haunting, unfamiliar chant of Matins and Compline; in between, she watched as mysterious, smiling women in dark habits glided up and down the worn wooden halls of the building, nodding their greetings to her, never speaking a word.

At first the silence nearly drove her insane. Like a person imprisoned in a soundproof chamber, she panicked at the irregular sounds of her own breathing, her heartbeat loud in her ears. Gradually, about the evening of the third day, the quietness began to settle into her spirit, pushing out the nagging anxieties about home, the long "to do" lists that filled her mind, emptying her heart of all thoughts but one: the longing to hear the Voice.

As Janelle continued to stare down toward the river, the door behind her opened, and a young novice entered, quiet as the morning fog. She carried a breakfast tray and fresh linens. Janelle whirled and looked at her intently, and the young woman raised a vulnerable, innocent face to meet her gaze. No word was spoken, but an expression of deep love and radiant joy filled the younger woman's eyes—the look of a girl in love. She smiled gently, peacefully at Janelle, then, setting her burden on the table, turned and left the room as silently as she had come.

Janelle lifted the lid on the breakfast tray. The standard fare: fresh fruit, home-baked wheat bread with butter, steaming oatmeal, a glass of milk. Five days without caffeine, salt, refined sugar, or red meat had generated a sense of physical well-being in her—a lightness of body, a healthy clearness of mind. In truth, she felt wonderful, better than she had in years. But still the silence prevailed.

As she ate, Janelle looked around at the Spartan quarters. Small, clean, and spare, its only furnishings were the desk and chair she used for meals and study, a narrow bed covered by a soft gray spread, and a tiny wardrobe which held her week's supply of clothing and personal necessities. The room was completely free of adornment except for a crucifix hanging against the whitewashed stucco over the bed.

Janelle had grown up believing that the crucifix was itself a kind of heresy—an icon of false belief. Christ didn't stay on the cross, after all: He died and was buried, and was raised up again on the third day. The empty cross was the symbol of his victory.

She sat down on the bed and reached up, taking down the crucifix and holding it in her lap. The cross itself, about ten inches in length, was crafted of fine walnut, hand-rubbed to a soft, dark sheen. The sculpture of Christ, cast in bronze, hung from the wood by small brass pins thrust through bored holes in the hands and feet.

Janelle fingered the crucifix absently, studying the detail on the figure of the small bronze Jesus. It wobbled a little, and the unexpected movement made her realize how lifelike the casting really was. The muscles in His arms stretched out in agonizing tautness; the calves of His legs cramped against the weight of his body bearing down upon them. Thin bronze rivulets of blood ran down into a tormented face, drawn by tiny, needle-sharp brass thorns pressing permanently into his temples.

Janelle shut her eyes against the pain, trying to block out the images of blood and noise and torture that threatened to overwhelm her. Had He truly done this, the Innocent One so brutally murdered, willingly offering His arms and legs and head and heart—not brass, but flesh and blood and screaming nerves and dislocated bones—for her?

She gasped, feeling a small pinprick of pain in the fleshy part of her left palm. Looking down, she saw with horror the brass figure of Christ lying in her lap and the cross, empty of its sculpture, gripped in her right hand. Imbedded in her left hand, one of the tiny brass nails stuck fast, drawing blood.

Janelle panicked. Would the nuns, who had offered their hospitality so graciously, think that she had deliberately vandalized the crucifix? She scrabbled around on the bed, searching desperately for the other two nails. At last she found them, and, propping the cross on her knees, proceeded to try to repair the damage she had done.

She managed to get the brass pins back into the holes, but the figure wouldn't hold. The cross was old; the wood must have dried, loosening the pins that held the sculpture of Christ. Urgently she pressed, trying to push the nails a little deeper into the wood. She gripped the feet with her left hand and pushed at the arms, one at a time.

Her palm, still bleeding, smeared red across the bronze feet of the recalcitrant Jesus. Janelle's fingers began to tremble. What on earth was she doing, trying to put Christ back on the cross?

Carefully, even tenderly, she laid the cross with its unsteady occupant on the bed next to her. Her hand streaked a little more blood onto the spread, and when she tried in vain to rub it off, she merely made the stain worse. Tears filled Janelle's eyes, and she heaved a long, ragged sigh. Now what?

Invisibly, imperceptibly, the presence she had longed for filled the room. She saw nothing, felt nothing, heard nothing. But somewhere, deep inside her, a door opened in a secret place she had never known before, and the words entered her heart:

You have tried in vain, my child, to offer yourself up as a sacrifice for me. But it will not work. You cannot replace me on the cross; all your blood and tears and sighing will never be enough.

"Then what is enough?" Janelle heard her own voice whisper, breaking the silence.

I am enough.

Janelle stared at the brass figure of the crucified

Christ. The expression on the face looked different, somehow—not tortured, or in agony, but at peace. Gently, with a wavering forefinger, she traced the arms reaching outward, the legs stretching down.

"But you have seemed so far away, Lord," she said at last, her tears spilling over.

I have been near, the Voice answered within her. *Silent, but near.*

A question rose up, but Janelle choked it back. She could not ask why; she would not.

The answer came anyway. *There is a time to speak, and a time to keep silent. You needed my silence more than you needed a sense of my presence.*

This time Janelle determined to ask the question aloud. "Why, Lord?"

Sin did not separate you from me, the Voice responded, *nor did you need to work to prove your worthiness. You have remained faithful when I have been silent, and I am pleased.*

A warmth spread through Janelle, infusing her with a sense of fulfillment. She hadn't imagined the silence; she had only misinterpreted it.

For a long time she sat on the bed, not praying, not seeking any other word. Silence engulfed her again, but this time it was not the silence of isolation, but of unspoken companionship. At last she picked up the cross and tried once more to replace the figure of the crucified Lord; this time it held. Tenderly, with a new sense of reverence, she hung it once more over the bed.

Janelle walked to the open window and looked down once more at the cornfield bordering the river.

It was nearly noon. The sun had risen high and shone on the golden grain with a bright, reflective light. The wind had shifted, and from far below she heard clearly the crash of the river against the rocks and the piercing call of the white gulls hanging on the wind.

&

Medicine Man

And Jesus said to them, "Surely you will quote this proverb to me: 'Physician, heal yourself!'"
—Luke 4:23

FOR THE FIRST TIME in months, the news around Turner's Crossroads had made the front page of the *Angstrom County Chronicle:* **FAMED MAYO DOCTOR TO SET UP PRACTICE IN TURNER'S CROSSROADS**.

The story had come out in Thursday's paper, but as usual the scoop had broken long before at the Four Korners Kafe. The grapevine was much more efficient than the UP wire service; for a week everybody in town had been speculating on the renowned medical man who had decided to opt for the simpler life of a small-town family physician.

"I just don't get it," Marvin Angstrom said over his third cup of coffee. "Why does a guy like this want to come here?" He drummed his fingers across the headline and furrowed his brow.

"Maybe he needs the money," Eddie Bjerke gibed, laughing at his own joke. The Crossroads Clinic and Hospital was notorious for underpayment of its medical team; even though the days were long gone when physicians were paid with chickens and sweet corn, the clinic still had a difficult time keeping qualified doctors on staff. In the past two years, three of the five physicians had left for greener pastures in Minneapolis and Rapid City, and a fourth, the decrepit old Herbert Helgeson, would have been forced into retirement had the situation not been so desperate.

"Nah," Johnny Leland said, lowering his voice to a conspiratorial whisper, "I think the guy's got some skeleton in his closet—otherwise, why would this Mayo Genius take a job lancing boils on the backside of nowhere? It's probably malpractice for leaving a scalpel in some senator's wife, or maybe a scandal involving two or three nurses—"

"I think you've got a skeleton rattling around in your brain," Mavis Kitchens said caustically, snatching the plate of donuts from the center of the table. "No more sugar for you, Johnny—your imagination's on overload."

The others laughed, and Johnny Leland flushed red. Mavis poured another round of coffee and drew herself up to her full height of five-four. "It's *my* opinion," she said regally, like a queen passing judgment on a court of fools, "that we're lucky to be getting a doctor like Andre DeLaval in Turner's Crossroads. He's supposed to be one of the finest internists in the state, and—"

A chorus of hoots and boos silenced her. "What do you know about *internists*, Mavis?" Eddie said, winking at the guys around the table. "Besides, Rochester is the biggest, best hospital in the country. If this new doctor is such a prima donna, why is he coming here?"

Mavis glared down at him and raised one eyebrow. "Maybe he's heard about my homemade pie," she said, then turned her back and glided royally back to the counter.

Eddie poked Johnny Leland in the arm. "I think Mavis has got a crush on the mystery doctor," he said, loud enough for her to hear. "She's in love with the idea of his being French—it's so *ro-mantic....*" He flashed a smile in Mavis's direction.

"He's not French," she said. "He's from New Orleans. He went to Tulane, finished first in his class, and got a prime residency at Mayo."

Eddie Bjerke rolled his eyes. "Ah, fellas, she *has* studied up on this gent!" he said. "How do you know so much about him, Mavis?"

Mavis picked up the newspaper from the counter and held it up so they could see the headlines. "I read," she said. "You should try it sometime."

❧

In truth, no one *needed* to read in order to know about Andre DeLaval's imminent arrival in Turner's Crossroads. The *Chronicle* gave the facts, but the gossip was much more interesting.

Christine Cameron, the real estate agent from Blue River Realty, told Betty Ruth Oleson, her hairdresser, who told her husband, Burt. Between Burt at the grain elevator and Betty Ruth at the beauty shop, the whole town heard the entire story in less time than it took for the *Angstrom County Chronicle* to set the type for the headline.

Andre DeLaval, the reputed Golden Boy of Rochester, had, according to rumor, become disenchanted with the hurried, harried medical machinery at the Mayo Clinic. As his residency drew to a close, he was first on the list to be offered a coveted staff position at the great hospital, but much to his chief of staff's dismay, turned the offer down flat.

Andre DeLaval, according to Christine Cameron via Betty Ruth and Burt Oleson, actually *wanted* a small-town practice, where he could get to know his patients on a first-name basis. He appreciated the slower, simpler pace of the Midwest; he actually, of all unheard-of things, *liked* the long, slow, snowy winters, and he wanted to settle down in a small community where he didn't have to live for his practice, where he could put down roots and live in peace.

And so, with the recommendation of the chief of staff at Mayo, he had signed on, sight unseen, with the medical team of the clinic in Turner's Crossroads.

"So, tell me," Betty Ruth asked, taking her time with Christine's hair so she could pump her for more information, "what does this new doctor *look* like?"

Christine craned her neck around and gave Betty Ruth a sidelong glance. "That's the strangest part," Christine said. "I've never seen the man."

"But I thought you sold him a house."

"Not *a* house," Christine corrected. "*The* house—the Willstead place, all twelve acres and a hundred thousand dollars worth."

Betty Ruth let out a low whistle. The Willstead home was a showplace in Turner's Crossroads—a nearly new brick ranch home, sprawling out in every direction on the top of an elegant hill just north of town. The lush green lawn sloped downward into woods on three sides, and the Blue River ran adjacent to the property.

The home itself had five bedrooms and two fireplaces, and an enormous master bath with a heart-shaped whirlpool tub. Jarvis Willstead, the banker, had had it custom-built three years before to show off his money, then never occupied it. Before he could close on the escrow, the FDIC investigators found some significant discrepancies in Willstead's bookkeeping and had carted him off to take up residence in the state penitentiary. The house had sat empty since then, a glorious monument to the juiciest scandal in the history of Turner's Crossroads.

"Even at a hundred thousand, the property was quite a steal," Christine said. "No pun intended." She laughed and turned her head, trying to see the back of her hair.

"Go on, go on," Betty Ruth prodded impatiently.

"Well, then, a couple of months ago, I got a call from this lawyer in Rochester, representing DeLaval. Everything was on the up and up; I checked. But the whole deal has been handled through the lawyer. I've never seen the doctor or his family."

"He has a family?"

"Two children, ages five and seven," Christine affirmed. "And a wife who's supposed to be an absolute knockout."

"That's too bad," Betty Ruth said.

"What's too bad?"

"His wife, the knockout," Betty Ruth answered. "Poor Mavis Kitchens will be crushed."

❧

Mavis wasn't crushed, exactly, although she did secretly admit to a mild disappointment at finding out that Andre DeLaval was married. But she was a strong woman, strong enough to laugh at her own foolish fantasies of being swept up and carried away from a life of waitressing by a dashing, handsome young doctor. In place of that illusion, she pictured herself striking up a friendship with the doctor's knockout wife—a tall, willowy blonde with her hair piled up in a French knot and diamonds dangling from her ears—and being drawn into the higher social echelons of Angstrom County. In this secondary dream, Mavis imagined herself thrown together with DeLaval's best friend and medical partner, and *he* fell madly in love with her.

Mavis looked around at the crowd gathered for afternoon coffee at the Four Korners and listened to snatches of their conversation. Apparently she wasn't the only one in Turner's Crossroads who entertained fantasies about the Mystery Man.

The fact that no one had seen him did not in the least dampen the enthusiasm for conjecture. Based on his French name, his apparent financial stability, and his medical reputation, the women tended to cast him as tall, dark, and handsome—for the younger women, an image of Mel Gibson in a white lab coat; for the older generation, a Victor Mature or a Tyrone Power.

The men came up with a different interpretation. Some, like the cynical Johnny Leland, insisted that there was something dark and shady lurking in the doctor's past, some unrevealed secret that forced him into an isolated practice in a town with little to offer except creative gossip. Others, with a more generous bent to their nature, concluded that he must be the lost heir to the DeLaval Cream Separator fortune, a man whose philanthropic heart and vast inheritance allowed him the luxury of practicing medicine for the pure joy of helping people.

They were all immersed in speculation when the door to the Four Korners Kafe open. It was the voice—the rich baritone with just a slight hint of a Southern accent—that startled them to silence.

"Pardon me," the voice rumbled, "but can anyone direct me to the offices of Blue River Realty?"

All heads turned. Framed in the doorway stood a short, slight man in a sports coat and tie. The afternoon sun glared behind him so that his feature were shrouded in shadow. No one moved; no one spoke.

At last Mavis Kitchens found her voice. "Please, come in," she stammered.

"Thank you," the voice answered. He shut the door gently behind him, cutting off the sun's rays. "I am the new doctor at the clinic. Andre DeLaval."

Mavis nodded dumbly as the man walked across

the cafe and extended his hand over the counter.

Andre DeLaval was black.

ॐ

"Well, it seems there was one fact about the renowned Dr. DeLaval that his uptown lawyer failed to mention," Betty Ruth Oleson snapped as she jerked viciously at Christine Cameron's hair.

"It wasn't relevant," Christine repeated for the fifth time, wincing as Betty Ruth snagged the brush in the tender hair at the nape of her neck. "Equal housing, and all that. You know how the government regulations are." She sighed. "Besides," she went on resolutely, "I don't care if the man is purple. His money's just as green as everybody else's."

"Is that all you can think about, your precious commission?" Betty Ruth said.

"In the case of the Willstead place, it is a pertinent consideration," Christine replied. "And what, I ask you, is the big deal? We do have other black people living in Turner's Crossroads, you know."

"Not in the ritziest house in town," Betty Ruth snorted.

"The man's a *doctor*, for heaven's sake!"

"Exactly. And this *doctor* has come to town expecting that we'll just fall all over ourselves getting in line for appointments to see him." She shuddered. "Now you tell me, Christine, can you *imagine* the men in this town allowing their wives and daughters to be intimately examined by a *black* doctor?"

Christine sighed. "I hear his credentials are impeccable," she said lamely.

"So what?" Betty Ruth replied. "Nobody is going to care about his credentials. I, for one, would rather die than let the likes of him touch me."

ɾ

Although most did not express their emotions as directly as Betty Ruth Oleson did, many of the long-time residents of Turner's Crossroads seemed to share her attitude. With true Scandinavian reticence, they kept their feelings to themselves.

"What about that new doctor?"

"Well, I don't know. It really is something, him moving here and all."

"Yep, it's something, all right."

Johnny Leland listened to this non-discussion until he could stand no more. He was only part Norwegian, after all, and the taint of the Irish from his mother's background often demonstrated itself in his temper.

"I told you!" he said to Mavis Kitchens as she poured coffee for the regular crowd at the Four Korners Kafe. "Didn't I tell her, Marv?"

Marvin Angstrom looked up from stirring his coffee. "Tell her what?"

"I told her that this mystery doctor was hiding something."

"You said he'd probably been sued for malpractice," Eddie Bjerke put in.

"Never mind that," Johnny sputtered. "Well, he was hiding something, all right—something he can't hide any more, now that he's here!"

"What are you getting so heated up about, Johnny?"

Marv asked. "So. The man's black. And he's a doctor. A black doctor."

"Yeah, that's something, all right," Eddie said.

"Just shut up, will you, Eddie?" Johnny snarled. He turned on Marv. "Well, Marv, what about it?"

"What about what?"

"You're so laid-back about the whole thing. Are you going to let this Mayo wonder-boy work on you? Are you going to take your *wife* to see him?"

Marv glared at Johnny as if offended that he would bring Addie into this discussion. The pigeon had come home to roost, and he couldn't avoid giving an answer. He looked down at his coffee cup, then back up at Johnny Leland's challenging gaze.

"I don't know, Johnny," he said morosely. "I just don't know."

❧

Apparently, most of the people in Turner's Crossroads *didn't* know, and couldn't make up their minds. When the flu epidemic hit, they stayed away in droves, or called the clinic to make specific appointments with the ancient Dr. Helgeson, who could barely get around to them all. Dr. Stearns, who had been at the clinic for a few years but was never very popular because of his lack of bedside manner, also gleaned a few of the sickest ones—until he contracted the virus himself and took to his bed for three weeks. Some, in utter desperation, even called old Doc Henley, who had been retired for years and was no longer licensed to practice in the state.

Standard Brown and her son, Regis, drove several

of the lower town residents in to the clinic for antibiotics. But except for that handful of black patients and one out-of-state driver who fell asleep at the wheel and broke his leg when his car hit a bridge abutment, Dr. Andre DeLaval was consigned to reorganizing the drug cabinets and changing the linens in the emergency room.

"I just don't understand it," he said, pacing back and forth across the expanse of the sunken living room in the former Willstead home. "I'm a good doctor; I've got years of experience, and—" He flopped down on the white sofa, sighing deeply.

"Well, I understand it perfectly," his wife, Lovey, interrupted, handing him a tall glass of iced tea. She wedged her rotund body onto the sofa beside him and reached over to loosen his tie. "It's got nothing to do with your expertise or your experience. It has to do with this—"

She picked up his hand and compared it with her own. Her skin, a deep chocolate brown, contrasted sharply with his lighter coffee-with-cream color. "Now, *that's* black," she laughed lightly, wiggling her own fingers. "But *this*—" She counted off his fingers, one by one. "Why, this is just a California tan." She sat up straight and looked at him seriously. "Do you know, Andre, that people pay good money and get skin cancer to have that kind of tan?"

He chuckled and pulled his hand from hers, stroking her gently on the side of her cheek. She was a wonder, his Lovey, with her dark clear skin and her intense black eyes and those lovely rounded curves in all the right places. She bewailed the fact that she outweighed him by forty pounds, but Andre never complained. She had a quick mind and a tender heart, and he adored her.

A shadow passed over Andre's face as he looked at his wife, and she saw it immediately.

"What's wrong, honey?"

He shook his head. "Nothing. Nothing. I was just thinking—"

"About what?"

"About you. About how you had begun to build a good client base with the real estate firm in Rochester. I know we said that once we got settled here, you'd pick up and start again, but given the situation here—"

She put a gentle hand to his lips. "Given the situation here," she said, "I think we'd better just not worry about it right now." She smiled. "If it happens, it happens. If it doesn't, well, then...something else will. When God shuts a door, He opens a window."

His mouth twisted in a wry smile. "Another wise saying from your sainted grandmother?"

She laughed. "A quote from *The Sound of Music*. But it's true, nevertheless."

He drew her close in a long embrace. "I wish I had your faith," he murmured.

She drew back and looked at him. "You do, Andre," she said with conviction.

He leaned over to kiss her, but was interrupted by the sound of the front door slamming, followed by high-pitched giggles and the slap of little feet against the marble floor in the entryway.

"Daddy! Daddy!" two little girls squealed as they dashed into the living room and flung themselves onto the sofa between their parents. The smallest one grabbed her mother's hand and began to pull. "Y'all gotta come see!"

"Slow down, Renfroe!" Andre said, laughing. "Come see what?" He turned to his eldest. "Ramona, what happened to you?"

The two girls stood up and faced him, jostling each other. Ramona had mud and grass smeared on both knees of her jeans, and Renfroe's hair stood out in all directions, littered with twigs and leaves.

"We saw a rabbit, Daddy—in our own yard!" Ramona said.

"And a peasant!" Renfroe added.

Ramona gave her a look of disdain. "A *pheasant*, idiot," she corrected.

"Don't call your sister names," Lovey said, an amused expression on her face. "You girls look like a disaster waiting to happen."

"I think it already happened," Andre said.

"Can we take a bath?" Renfroe asked suddenly.

Andre and Lovey exchanged a puzzled glance. Would wonders never cease—their daughters *asking* for a bath?

Ramona slanted a look at her little sister; clearly there was a conspiracy going on here. "In the heart-shaped tub," she added. *"Please?"*

Andre nodded to his wife and shrugged. "Y'all go ahead," he said. "I have to be back at the hospital in an hour."

Lovey gave him a questioning look. "Dr. Helgeson has been swamped," he explained. "So I get to man the emergency room." He cocked an eyebrow at her.

"I'll take a book along," he said. "It's bound to be a long, boring night."

Lovey herded the two girls down the hall toward the master bath, and Andre picked up his iced tea and took a long drink, sighing. He had chosen Turner's Crossroads so he could have more free time with Lovey and the girls. But he had never expected to be completely idle. And he couldn't survive without patients for long.

When the door chimes rang, Andre couldn't place the sound. He looked up at the clock, and then at the telephone. The chimes sounded again—a Westminster sequence, like the grandfather clock in his father's study. At last, realizing the source, he strode to the door and opened it.

On the porch stood a thin, wispy-looking woman dressed in a white cotton blouse and a navy skirt and jacket. She wore round gold-rimmed glasses over her striking blue eyes, and she smiled up at him, waiting.

"May I help you?" he said at last.

"Dr. DeLaval? I am Sister Gertrude Hoffstadt, of the St. Sebaldus convent and school."

"Yes?" Andre still stood holding onto the door, his outstretched arm blocking the entrance.

"May I come in for a moment?" the nun said.

Andre came to his senses. "Oh...certainly, come in," he faltered.

"Am I interrupting something?" Sister Gertrude asked.

"Not at all," he said, recovering his composure. "Forgive my rudeness; we just...well, we just haven't had many visitors."

"So I understand." She followed him into the living room and accepted his offer of iced tea.

"My wife is bathing the children," he said when she had settled herself in a chair adjacent to the couch. "She'll be out shortly."

"I'll get right to the point," Sister Gertrude said, looking directly into his eyes. "You haven't had a very resounding welcome here in Turner's Crossroads, as I understand it."

He shook his head. "I'm afraid not. But then, people have to be given time to adjust, to—"

"There's no excuse for it," the nun interrupted, her eyes blazing. "It's bigotry, pure and simple. I would have been here sooner, except that I have been out of town on parish business—"

He held up a hand. "Sister, I hardly expected a welcoming committee from the Catholic church."

Her blue eyes pierced him, and she smiled—a warm, genuine smile. "And I am hardly a committee. I must tell you that there are people in our parish who bear some decidedly unchristian attitudes toward your presence here in Turner's Crossroads."

She paused, and her nose wrinkled as if she had caught a whiff of dead skunk. "But St. Sebaldus stands on the example of Christ," she went on, "and Father O'Connell has made it clear that you and your family *will* be welcome in our church."

"Even if your parishioners don't agree?"

"Even so. Some principles are not negotiable. This is one of them."

Andre smiled broadly. "That is very kind of you, Sister. But my family and I—"

"Are not Catholic," she finished for him.

He shook his head ruefully. "Lutheran."

The nun's eyes widened. "You're kidding."

"It's not so unusual where I come from. There aren't many Lutheran churches in New Orleans, but a number of them serve the black community. You'd be surprised how many non-Baptist blacks there are in the South."

"Do you intend to attend St. Thomas?" Sister Gertrude asked.

He thought for a moment, running his fingers around his iced tea glass. "We...ah, haven't been to any services since we arrived," he hedged.

"Well," she said briskly, "we're not in the business of proselytizing, but please know that you are welcome to worship with us at St. Sebaldus any time."

"Thank you, Sister," he said. "That means more than you can know."

"I have had a little firsthand experience with prejudice," she responded. "There is significant anti-Catholic sentiment abroad as well."

She stood to leave, shaking his hand warmly. "Catholic or not," she said as she paused in the doorway, "Father O'Connell has extended an invitation for you and your wife to have dinner with him at the rectory."

"Will you be there?" Andre asked. Oddly, he wished she would be. Lovey and this nun would have a lot in common.

"Indeed I will," she said. "I wouldn't miss it for the world."

❧

At one-fifteen a.m., Dr. Andre DeLaval sat dozing in a chair at the Emergency Room desk, a battered copy of Baldwin's *Native Son* in his lap.

When the telephone rang, he jerked awake, his heart pounding, and dropped the book to the floor. Snatching up the receiver, he shouted "Yes! Hello?"

"This is Sheriff Ferrel," said the voice on the other end. It was a bad connection; the man sounded distant, as if under water. "You've got an ambulance coming your way—arriving in about five minutes, and—" The phone sputtered, and the line went dead.

Andre clicked the receiver button several times, but there was no connection. He buzzed the intercom and said, "Send me a nurse and an aide—right now!"

By the time the doors to the hospital wing swung open, admitting a slow-moving, heavy-set woman in white and a pimply-faced young man of about twenty, Andre could already see the flashing lights of the ambulance as it turned into the parking lot. "Get a gurney," he commanded. He turned on his heel and dashed for the outer doors.

The paramedics had the stretcher out of the ambulance and into the hallway before Andre could take stock of the situation. "Abdominal pains," one of the technicians said. "Looks like a ruptured appendix."

"Get her into Room 1," Andre snapped. He turned to the lumbering nurse who was pushing a bare gurney slowly down the hall. "Get me a gown," he said. "And prepare for OR."

The woman's eyes widened. "We're going to operate? Now? Here?"

A rough hand jerked Andre around, and he found himself facing a tall, lanky man in blue jeans and a disheveled pajama top. A shock of blond hair fell into his eyes, and he pushed it back impatiently. "No you're not," the man said, his voice low and his eyes narrowed as he surveyed Andre. "You're not touching my wife."

Andre had seen the man before—that first day in the Four Korners Kafe, and afterward on the street. Always the man had given him that same scrutinizing look—suspicious, spiteful.

"What is your name, sir?" Andre asked in a level tone.

"Leland—Johnny Leland."

"And your wife?"

"Corinne." One word, no more. The man stood like a statue, legs braced, arms crossed.

"Mr. Leland," Andre said, watching out the corner of his eye as the nurse lumbered into overdrive, preparing the operating room, "if I don't operate—now—your wife may die."

Johnny Leland's sunburned face blanched, but he stood his ground. "Call Helgeson—or Stearns."

"Dr. Stearns is still in bed with the flu," Andre said. "And Dr. Helgeson is not up to it."

"He'll be up to it," Johnny said. "Call him."

"You call him," Andre said shortly. "I have a patient to attend to."

Johnny Leland bolted for the telephone, and Andre disappeared into the operating room.

☙

Forty-five minutes later, a bleary-eyed, trembling Herbert Helgeson staggered into the Emergency Room. Johnny Leland met him at the door.

"It's Corinne, Doc," he said. "She's—she's real bad. They say it's a ruptured appendix, and they've got to operate—"

Dr. Helgeson stared up at him, uncomprehending. "I...I can't do it, Johnny," he stammered. "My eyes...they're just not good enough. And my hands—" He held out a withered, age-spotted hand and watched as it shook like a dry leaf in a high wind.

"You've got to do it!"

Dr. Helgeson shook his head. "I'm sorry, Johnny."

Johnny Leland sank into a chair and dropped his head into his hands, repeating over and over, "Corinne! Corinne!"

A hand clenched Johnny's shoulder, and he looked up into the face of Merlin Logemann, pastor of St. Thomas Lutheran.

"Hello, pastor," Johnny managed, staring vacantly at Merle's face as if seeing nothing.

"Sheriff Ferrel called me," Merle said simply. "He thought you might need a friend."

Johnny nodded mutely. "Corinne..." he began.

"I know," the pastor answered quietly.

"I—I wouldn't let him operate, and now..."

"It'll be all right, Johnny," Logemann answered, trying to sound confident. "Maybe we should pray about it."

Johnny nodded and bowed his head. Pastor Logemann prayed, quietly, earnestly.

When the prayer was ended, Johnny opened his eyes on a pair of tan trousers and the lower half of a white coat, a stethoscope dangling from the pocket. He raised his head; it was Dr. Andre DeLaval, the object of his anger, looking down at him with an expression of compassion. Suddenly Johnny saw, not a black man, but a doctor, a professional, the Genius of Mayo, who might have been able to save his wife if he had not been so stupid, so proud. Those deep brown eyes penetrated his own with a gaze of understanding.

"I'm sorry, Mr. Leland—" the doctor began.

Johnny gritted his teeth and heaved a great ragged sigh. "It was my fault, Doc," he said. "If I had just let you operate, Corinne might still be alive. She might still..."

The doctor shot a sidelong glance at Merlin Logemann, who had his arm around Johnny's shoulders, supporting him.

"Mr. Leland—Johnny," he said, gripping Johnny's arm with surprising strength for so small a man, "your wife is very much alive."

Johnny stared at him as if he didn't understand. "Alive? But—"

Dr. DeLaval shook his head. "I operated without your permission. I'm sorry. Technically I shouldn't have done it, but—"

"Alive?" Johnny shouted. "Is she...will she be all right?"

"She'll be just fine," the doctor said. "There was no time to spare, I'll admit. It was a close call. But your Corinne is a strong woman." He glanced at his watch. "They'll take her up to her room in a few minutes."

Johnny Leland stared for a moment at Dr. DeLaval.

The man was a full head shorter than himself, with close-cut black hair and skin the color of Mavis Kitchens's caramel pie. Johnny looked him up and down, then laughed out loud and did the unthinkable—he threw his arms around the doctor and hugged him hard.

It only lasted a fraction of a second. Johnny pulled back and grinned sheepishly, then stared down at the floor. "Sorry, Doc, I...uh, I just got carried away."

"It's quite all right, Johnny." Dr. DeLaval put out his hand and gave Johnny's a firm shake. "Now, if you don't mind coming into the office, there are some permission papers you'll need to sign."

❧

On Sunday morning, at the close of the service, Pastor Merlin Logemann came down from the altar and stood at the front of the aisle.

"We have a special joy today," he said as the members of his congregation glanced curiously at one another. "Our church family is about to be extended."

He motioned to the back of the church, and all heads turned as Dr. Andre DeLaval made his way down the aisle, flanked by a dark, smiling, rotund woman and two little girls in matching pink dresses. A murmuring wave followed them to the front of the sanctuary.

Merlin Logemann turned the DeLavals around to face the congregation. The two girls squirmed and grinned bashfully at the sea of white faces. "This," Pastor Logemann said, laying a hand on Andre's shoulder, "is Dr. Andre DeLaval, our new doctor in town." He laid the other hand on Lovey's broad back. "And this is his wife, Lovey."

A titter ran through the crowd as the pastor spoke her name, but he ignored it. "These are their daughters, Ramona and Renfroe." The two little girls craned their necks upward to look at his face, then giggled at him.

The pastor looked out over the congregation and frowned. Expressions of confusion and anger greeted his gaze. "Dr. DeLaval was raised in the Lutheran church. In New Orleans, he and his family were members of Our Savior's, and in Rochester, members of Trinity Lutheran." He paused and watched for a moment, then went on. "The DeLavals have expressed their desire to transfer their membership to St. Thomas. And," he finished emphatically, "they *will* be received with the right hand of fellowship and the acceptance of Christ's love."

A rumble of dissent ran through the congregation, and then their attention was diverted by a movement near the back of the sanctuary.

Johnny Leland unfolded his lanky frame from the pew, straightened his jacket, and cleared his throat. All eyes fixed on him as he came down the aisle and stood beside Andre DeLaval.

"You all know how I felt about DeLaval coming to doctor in Turner's Crossroads," he said, fidgeting with his tie. "Well, I was wrong. And I'm proud to stand with him today and welcome him into this church." He put an arm around the doctor's shoulder and squeezed hard.

For the first time since the day of Manny Fisher's

baptism, St. Thomas Lutheran church was completely silent. Johnny Leland stood there, glancing around uncertainly, until he felt an insistent tug on the sleeve of his jacket.

He looked down. There stood Renfroe, the younger of the little DeLavals, gazing at him with an expression of wonder and trust, holding her little arms up to him.

Johnny squatted down and picked her up. She gave him a quick, fierce hug, then turned around in his arms and surveyed the ocean of white faces that stared up at her.

For a moment the child watched, wide-eyed. Then she gave a broad, sweet-faced smile and waved to the congregation, batting her eyelashes. "Hi, y'all," she said timidly.

And everybody laughed.

ॐ

Verlys Bakke's First Confession

Therefore confess your sins to each other and pray for each other so that you may be healed.
—James 5:16

VERLYS BAKKE STOOD at the show window of Harv Hanson's Buick dealership, looking very much like a small boy pressing his nose against the glass of a candy counter. He was, after all, drooling over a kind of adult jawbreaker: a bright red Sunbird convertible, its top thrown back to reveal seductive white leather interior and burled woodgrain dashboard.

Painted on the windshield with white liquid shoe polish was the tongue-in-cheek advertisement: MID-LIFE SPECIAL; E-Z TERMS AVAILABLE!

Through the glare of the window, Verlys suddenly caught a glimpse of Harv's round, red face peering at him with a knowing grin. *Come on in.* Harv's fleshy lips mouthed the words soundlessly—an overweight Valentino in a silent movie.

As if caught in an indecent act, Verlys jerked his raincoat shut and shook his head. He turned and hurried away, but not before he saw himself reflected in the glass—a pale, balding man in horn-rimmed glasses and a ten-year-old suit that bulged slightly around the middle.

It was not a pretty picture, this unforgiving glimpse of himself as he was at fifty-three. Verlys had always wanted more for himself; in his youth, when he had a full head of hair and ambitions for greatness, he had envisioned a life of success and acclaim, hobnobbing with the movers and shakers of the great Midwest, flying off to Chicago and Miami and New York to close business deals with the rich and famous.

Instead, he had resigned himself to a secure middle-management position at Midwestern Telecom, overseeing the boring, redundant business of assembling parts for cellular telephones. Twice a year he drove his battered Chevy to the Greater Midwestern Electronics Symposium in Minneapolis; once, five years ago, he and his wife, Una, had made the trip to Wisconsin Dells and spent one day getting a sunburn and the next three trying to stay out of the rain.

Verlys sighed and slipped into the Chevy. He banged the door hard, and it sprang back on its hinges. Three bangs later, it finally shut. The old V-8 roared to life, spewing a cloud of blue smoke into the air behind it.

Verlys leaned on the steering wheel and sighed.

Why, God, does life never turn out the way we plan it?

❧

"Bad day, Verlys?"

The voice startled Verlys, and he jerked his head up, bumping his bald spot on the low-slung roof. He looked up to see Pastor Merlin Logemann leaning in the passenger window.

"Merle—I...I didn't hear you."

"I'm not surprised," the pastor said. "I doubt you can hear anything over the roar of this antique." He laughed and pounded the palm of his hand on the windshield of the car.

"Yeah, I guess I'm due for a new muffler."

"Or maybe a new car," Merle suggested.

An image flashed across Verlys's mind: *An open country road, with the red convertible spitting up dust behind it, himself at the wheel, the wind blowing in his hair....*

Verlys reached up self-consciously and smoothed his long side hairs over his bald spot. "So, what's up, Pastor?" he said, not meeting Merle's eyes.

"Not you, I'd bet," Merle answered. "You look like the head cheerleader just turned you down for a date to the Prom."

Verlys glared at him. "Not funny, Pastor."

Merle smiled and shook his head. "Sorry. But you do look like you could use a friend. Want to go have coffee and talk?"

Verlys's foot slipped, and he accidentally gunned the engine. He hadn't meant to, but the result was effective. Pastor Logemann took his hands off the car and stepped back onto the sidewalk.

"I guess not," he said. Then he leaned down and looked directly into Verlys's eyes. "We've been friends for a long time," he said. "Going on twelve years." Merle bit his lip and grimaced. "I know when something's eating at you."

Verlys attempted a lame smile. "I'm OK, Pastor, really I am. Just got a lot on my mind. We'll talk soon, all right?"

"Sure." Pastor Logemann straightened up and patted the side of the car with his hand. "See you, Verlys."

Verlys watched in the rearview mirror as Merle walked on down the sidewalk and disappeared into the Four Korners Kafe. Then, letting out a heavy sigh, he dropped the Chevy into gear and headed out of town.

☙

At seven-thirty that night, when Verlys wheeled into the gravel parking lot of the Roadside Inn, halfway between Marshall Forks and Portageville, he found himself looking around to see if he recognized any of the cars. He didn't. But suddenly he realized his paranoia as a sure sign of guilt.

And what, he thought, *do I have to be guilty about?* He wasn't doing anything wrong—not really. Just a simple dinner with a friend...an incredibly attractive young woman friend. Juliana Winnaker was new in town, hired as executive secretary to the president at Midwest Telecom. It was almost his duty to help her get acquainted, to feel less lost and lonely. Practically part of his job.

And she did, he had to admit, make him feel something he hadn't felt in years: special, somehow; important.

Then why had he lied to Una—simple, uncomplicated Una who trusted him implicitly and never doubted for a moment that he was, truly, having dinner with some "business associates." And why had he chosen this place, miles from nowhere, instead of the Cattle Car, where the food was better and the prices lower?

Verlys knew why, but he shoved the answer aside and determined that, for once, he was going to enjoy himself. He stopped at the black glass entrance to the Roadside Inn and checked his reflection in the door. The new tweed blazer made his graying hair look rather distinguished. He straightened his lapels and looked down at his gray leather boots, also new. They gave him a couple of extra inches of height and made him feel slightly rebellious, in a swaggering, free-wheeling, James-Dean sort of way. Satisfied, he pulled the door open and strode into the dimly lit supper club.

Juliana was waiting for him in the back booth, her auburn hair glowing in the candlelight. She turned her face up toward him as he slid in opposite her, puckering her lips in a pretended pout. "You're late," she whined, her long fingers inching across the table toward his hand like a red-footed spider crawling toward its prey.

He jerked his hand back before the spider reached him and ran a nervous finger around his too-tight collar. "I...uh, sorry," he said, glancing around. "It just took me longer to drive out here than I thought."

"Yes," she breathed, "but it's worth it, isn't it?" She raised one eyebrow, as if the question held great significance.

"Did you order?"

"Of course not, silly," she said, giving a high-pitched laugh. "I waited for you."

Verlys grabbed for the menu and opened it, grateful for a diversion from her penetrating gaze. But before he had the time to scan through "Steaks" to "Seafood," the spider-hand inched over the top of the menu and pushed it aside.

"Let's dance," she said.

For the first time, Verlys realized that the center of the restaurant was dominated by a dance floor, the old neon-lighted disco kind, with pulsing strobes of color that turned the dancers into a macabre assortment of jerking, disconnected body parts. The band was playing a Beatles tune, nearly unrecognizable in its arrangement, with a head-pounding bass line and a wild, discordant lead. For an instant, Verlys remembered hearing such music in his own home, and yelling at his kids to turn the volume down.

"Great band, huh?" Juliana shouted over the din.

Verlys nodded.

"So, let's do it!" Juliana edged out of the booth and grabbed his nearest hand in both of hers, pulling at him.

"No...I...I'm not very good at that—" He waved his hand helplessly.

The pout returned, and Juliana flopped back into the booth.

"So then," Verlys said, attempting to redeem the

evening, "what do you feel like having?"

She smiled wickedly and arched her eyebrows. "What I *feel* like having, I probably can't have," she giggled.

"I was referring to the food," Verlys said. Her gaze made him acutely uncomfortable, but the attention was flattering. "We can talk about other things later."

"Yeah," she said, winking at him. "Dessert comes *after* dinner, doesn't it?"

ð

Verlys waited until Juliana had pulled out of the parking lot before making his way to his battered old Chevy. For a long time he sat with the window rolled down, looking at the almost-full moon and drinking in the cool night air.

The sounds of the band, still going strong, wafted out across the darkness, stirring in Verlys a painful, delicious sense of longing. This evening had been wine and vinegar, heady liberty and nagging guilt. But even the guilt gave him a sense of freedom, like a child running away from home, or a teenager staying out after curfew. There might be a day of reckoning to come, but for now...for now, the young, adventurous, ambitious Verlys Bakke had been resurrected.

The honk of a car horn drew Verlys back to the present. There, right in front of him, leaning out the window with a perplexed look on his face, sat Merlin Logemann.

ð

On Sunday morning, Verlys made a weak excuse about not feeling well and sent Una off to church by herself. He made coffee and tried to read the paper, but his mind kept coming back to the image of Merle in the parking lot of the Roadside Inn.

What on earth was the pastor doing there, way out in the middle of nowhere on a Friday night? Worse than that, what did Merle think *he* was doing there? Had he been in the restaurant, seen Verlys with Juliana, watched them from the other side of the room? Had he seen how Juliana played with Verlys's fingers, sneaked French fries from his plate, hung on his arm when they finally rose to leave?

Did he notice the new tweed jacket and the gray leather cowboy boots?

Verlys sighed and flung the newspaper to the floor. He got up and paced across the living room and back again, muttering to himself. He looked at the clock: 11:45. Una wouldn't be home for several hours; there was a potluck dinner, and then a special Women's Circle meeting.

With a grunt, he plopped down on the couch and pulled on his boots. He didn't know where he was going, but he had to get out of this house.

❧

For an hour Verlys drove aimlessly through the countryside, down every back road and farm access, out to the highway, and back again. At last, almost without knowing it, he found himself in the parking lot of the Roadside Inn. *Returning to the scene of the crime,* he thought grimly.

The restaurant was closed, of course, locked up tight. Verlys could hardly believe it was the same place. In the broad light of day, he could see the peeling brown paint and the unmowed grass, the litter that caught in the rocks at the edge of the parking lot. He thought of Juliana, and found himself facing the memory, not of a tempting seductress, adoring him in the flower of his manhood, but a petulant child, demanding, manipulative.

Verlys walked up to the black glass doors and tried to peer in. All he could see was himself: a pasty, balding, middle-aged man with horn-rimmed glasses and a bulge around the middle, looking overfed and ridiculous in a tweed sports coat and new leather cowboy boots.

With a grunt of disgust, he turned on his heel, jumped into the Chevy, and spun away in a cloud of gravel dust and flying rock.

&

When Verlys got home, Una still had not returned. He took off his boots and changed into jeans and a sweatshirt, then walked out into the yard in his stocking feet, holding his tennis shoes in one hand.

The afternoon had turned chilly, and Verlys thought about going back inside to get a jacket. Instead, he sat down in the lawn swing and put on his shoes, gazing vacantly at the stone spires of St. Sebaldus Catholic Church.

Old Baldy, as the longtime residents of Turner's Crossroads called the church, had been there for nearly a century. Verlys had lived in the house next door for years, but, being a Lutheran, had never darkened the doors of the place. Somehow, without analyzing it, he had grown up feeling that even to enter such a place would be a betrayal of his faith, a denial of his Protestant heritage.

Yet now, as he sat there shivering in the swing, Verlys felt a compulsion to go inside St. Sebaldus, to see what was there. Perhaps he would be tainted forever by the smell of incense and the looming shadow of graven images rising up around him. Perhaps, as soon as he crossed the threshold, he would hear the crowing of a cock, as Peter did when he denied Christ the night of the crucifixion.

It was probably guilt—pure, unadulterated guilt—that made him get up and walk across the alley toward Old Baldy. He hadn't really *done* anything, not yet anyway, but he couldn't shake the memory of Merlin Logemann peering curiously at him in the parking lot of the Roadside Inn.

Holding his breath, Verlys stepped into the dark sanctuary of St. Sebaldus, jumping slightly as the heavy door clanged shut behind him. On either side of the altar, small votive candles burned, reminding him of Christmas candlelight services at St. Thomas Lutheran. Hanging directly behind the altar was an enormous crucifix, startlingly realistic in its agony. Verlys stared at it for a moment, then turned his eyes away.

He walked up a few rows and sat down, stumbling a bit as he kicked a kneeler that was still turned down after the morning Mass. Lutherans didn't kneel, at least not at St. Thomas, and his awareness of the kneeler, pressing against his ankles, made him wonder if he should do something—cross himself, or look around for some holy water.

"Welcome, my son."

The voice behind him caused him to flinch, and Verlys craned around to see a young-looking man in a black cassock standing behind him. He had the kind of boyish features that defied time; he could have been sixteen or thirty-six. But however old he was, the absurdity of being called *my son* almost caused Verlys to laugh out loud. The young priest picked up the incongruity immediately.

"Sorry," he said sheepishly, a faint pink tinge creeping up his neck. "I guess I've watched too many old Bing Crosby movies."

Verlys chuckled. Now, here was a priest to be reckoned with!

"I am Father John O'Connell," the priest said. "Can I help you in some way?"

"No, Pas—Father," Verlys said, correcting himself midstream. "I just came in to have a look around."

"Stay as long as you like." The young priest nodded slightly. "The house of God is open to all who seek Him."

Verlys opened his mouth to defend himself against this implicit accusation of faithlessness, to say, *I am a Christian; I am an elder in the Lutheran Church.* Then he shut it again. With a smile, the priest turned and glided silently up the aisle, pausing briefly to genuflect before the altar, then disappeared into a side door.

Verlys exhaled a long sigh and sank back into the pew, propping his feet on the kneeler. The stillness of the great vaulted nave descended over him, a palpable silence unlike anything Verlys had ever experienced. He sat there, quiet, for a long, long time—he didn't know how long—and waited.

What, exactly, was he waiting for? For God to descend and offer forgiveness for his waywardness? For the statue of the crucified Jesus to speak from the cross, as to the repentant thief at his side?

Verlys shut his eyes and waited some more. Behind his closed eyelids, he saw images that shamed him: a red convertible with MID-LIFE SPECIAL painted on the windshield; a spidery white hand with long red fingernails twining about his own; a tweed coat and a pair of cowboy boots; the face of Una, trusting, and Merlin Logemann, inviting him for coffee, wanting him to talk.

His eyes snapped open, his mind willing the images to go away. Then his gaze rested on a small card wedged between two prayer books in the hymn rack in front of him. He pried it out; it was a small brochure listing the ministries of St. Sebaldus and the timetable for Mass:

Masses Daily 7:00 a.m.
Saturday Mass 5:30 p.m.
Sunday Masses 8:30 a.m. and 10:30 a.m.
Confession Saturday afternoon, or by appointment

CONFESSION. Verlys's eyes riveted on the word. He had never been to confession, of course; he had only seen it done in movies. But he knew enough about it to realize that a priest was bound to utter confidentiality in confession. He could say anything...anything....

But could he? Could he tell a total stranger, even a priest, that he was sick of his job and sick of his bald spot and sick of his wife and completely frustrated with his entire life? Could he confess to this innocent-looking, boyish priest what a fool he'd been, and how guilty he felt for acting like such an idiot with that conniving, manipulating Juliana Winnaker?

Suddenly the truth struck him like a physical blow. He might be able get everything off his chest in one fell swoop—here, today, without anyone having to know. He could be free of the nagging guilt and the fear of discovery and go home to Una with a clear conscience. And he would never, never be such a fool again, he added as an afterthought.

Verlys jumped up from the pew like a man possessed, whacking his ankle hard against the kneeler. Gritting his teeth against the pain, he ran up the aisle and pounded on the side door.

Father O'Connell opened the door and peered out at the demented Protestant who stood banging as if he'd tear the place down.

"Father!" Verlys panted, standing on his good foot and holding his injured ankle up like an ungainly crane. "Father—can I—" He searched his memory for the right phrase. "Will you hear my confession?"

The priest's eyes widened with disbelief. "You are not a member of this church, are you?"

Verlys's face fell. "No...I'm a Lutheran, a member at St. Thomas." He left out the part about being an elder. "Do I have to be a Catholic to confess?"

The priest smiled—a gentle, indulgent boy-smile. "No, sir, but I thought you might prefer to speak to your own pastor..."

Verlys shook his head vehemently. "No, I...I need to get some things settled now. All right?"

"All right," the priest said. "Come into my office."

Verlys balked. *His office?* There was no way he could confess his sins if he had to look this boy in the eye. "Office?" he repeated stupidly. "Isn't there a...ah..."

"A confessional?" The young priest eyed Verlys intently. "Yes, we have a confessional. This is, after all, a very old church. But these days we rarely use it any more. Most confessions are offered more casually, face to face, in my office or in the chapel."

Verlys shook his head vehemently.

"We can use the confessional, if you prefer." Father O'Connell pointed toward the back of the sanctuary. "The door on the right."

"You mean that thing that looks like a phone booth?" Verlys blurted out.

The young man nodded. "I need to return to the rectory for a moment. You go ahead; I'll be with you shortly."

Relieved, Verlys limped back down the aisle and took his place in the confessional. He felt a little claustrophobic, but somehow just making the decision seemed to improve the situation immensely.

After a few moments he heard the door on the other side open and click shut again, but he could see nothing in the semi-darkness of the chamber.

"Father?" Verlys said. His throat was dry, and he licked his lips and tried to remember what he had seen in the movies. If he was going to go through with this, he wanted to do it the right way. It had to take the first time.

He took a deep breath. "Forgive me, Father, for I

have sinned," he stammered. "It has been...uh, I've never been to confession before in my life."

"That's all right," a voice whispered from the other side. "You're here now. What is it you wish to confess?"

Verlys began his confession—haltingly at first, then gaining momentum as he got into the swing of it. He began with his lust for the red car, then picked up the lie to Una, the boots, the dinner at the Roadside Inn, right on through to all his idiotic dreams of glory and his frustration with his mundane life in Turner's Crossroads. He even threw in a couple of flings during his stint in the Navy, just to set the record straight.

When he had finished, Verlys slumped against the seat of the confessional and uttered a deep sigh. He felt as if a huge burden had been lifted, and he flexed his shoulder muscles like an athlete cooling down after a workout.

"So what now, Father?" he said at last.

"Have you learned anything from this experience?" the voice asked.

"I sure have. I've been a complete fool, and I won't make the same mistakes again," Verlys answered with conviction. "I think I should learn to appreciate what I've got instead of wanting something I can't have."

"That sounds like a good plan," the voice said. "Your sins are forgiven. I will offer a prayer for you, and then you may go in peace."

"That's it?" Verlys said. "No penance? No Hail Marys?" This was not going right at all; surely there must be something he had to do.

"Nothing else," said the voice. "God's grace is sufficient for your forgiveness."

"Boy, that's a relief," Verlys said. "And nobody ever has to know?"

"No one but yourself and God." The voice offered a brief prayer, and then addressed Verlys. "Go in peace, and sin no more."

Verlys stretched his legs and stood up in the cramped quarters of the confessional. "Thank you, Father," he said.

"You're quite welcome, my son."

He opened the door and stepped into the stillness of the sanctuary, where he stood looking for a moment at the figure of Christ suspended on the cross. The face of Jesus seemed different...smiling, almost, as if He knew something Verlys didn't know.

Suddenly a movement below the crucifix caught his eye. There, at the base of the cross in front of the altar, knelt a young man in a black cassock, fingering his rosary as he prayed.

Verlys stared at the kneeling figure in disbelief. As he watched, Father O'Connell rose and faced him. "I'm sorry for the delay," he said, his soft voice echoing in the stillness of the nave. "I like to prepare myself before hearing confessions. You are ready?"

Verlys's mind spun wildly, and his heart pounded as if he had been running. *If this priest hadn't heard his confession, who had?*

"Has someone else been in here?" he demanded, his voice loud in the hush of the church.

"No, sir, not to my knowledge."

"Then who—?"

Verlys heard a noise behind him and jerked around. The outer door was swinging slowly shut, the creak of its hinges echoing into the shadows of the high ceiling. At last it closed with a resounding clang.

He dashed for the door and flung it open, peering into the gathering dusk. There was no one in sight, no sound except the soft twittering of birds and the bark of a dog in the distance. High above, perched on a wire, a gray dove cooed its sweet call into the twilight. *Who, who,* it sang.

Across the alley, the lights flickered on in the Bakkes' kitchen. Una was home, probably fixing leftovers for their Sunday night supper. He watched for a moment until he saw her familiar shadowy figure move past the window.

Verlys raised his eyes to the deepening sky, where one bright star glittered against the field of deep blue. The pounding of his heart slowed, and in his mind's eye he saw the figure of the crucified Jesus, larger than life, smiling down on him. *Who, who*, the dove repeated.

Verlys gazed up at the bird, and the peace he had felt before coursed into him like a flood. Maybe it didn't matter who. Maybe it didn't matter at all.

Shrugging, he shut the door gently behind him. Then he jogged across the alley, pausing only to give his battered Chevy an affectionate pat before taking the front steps two at a time.

❧